MILTON

being human
The Road

The **being human** *series from BBC Books:*

1. THE ROAD
by Simon Guerrier

2. CHASERS
by Mark Michalowski

3. BAD BLOOD
by James Goss

being human
THE ROAD

Simon Guerrier

Being Human is a Touchpaper TV production for BBC Three
Executive Producers: Toby Whithouse and Rob Pursey

Original series created by Toby Whithouse and broadcast on BBC Television.
'Being Human' and the Being Human logo are trademarks of the
British Broadcasting Corporation and are used under licence

10 9 8 7 6 5 4 3 2 1

Published in 2010 by BBC Books, an imprint of Ebury Publishing.
A Random House Group Company.

The Random House Group Ltd Reg. No. 954009.
Addresses for companies within the Random House Group can be found at
www.randomhouse.co.uk.

A CIP catalogue record for this book is available from the British Library.

ISBN 978 1 846 07898 9

The Random House Group Limited supports the Forest Stewardship Council
(FSC), the leading international forest certification organisation. All our titles
that are printed on Greenpeace approved FSC certified paper carry the FSC
logo. Our paper procurement policy can be found at www.rbooks.co.uk/
environment

Series Editor: Steve Tribe
Cover design by Lee Binding © Woodlands Books, 2010

Printed and bound in Great Britain by CPI Cox and Wyman, Reading, RG1 8EX

To buy books by your favourite authors and register for offers,
visit www.rbooks.co.uk

*For Simon Belcher
and all those
nights we tried
to take over
the world*

'Tea!' hollered Annie, over the noise of frying eggs. She reached for the spatula and deftly flipped each egg onto a waiting piece of toast. 'Food!' she yelled.

Above her, upstairs, the thud-thud-thud-*crash* meant the boys had got their shoes on. Then, *crash*-thud-thud-thud, they were both tumbling down the narrow staircase and clattering into the kitchen.

Annie wheeled round, presenting them both with tea and toast and egg.

'Wh-what?' flustered George, blinking at her from behind fragile, frameless glasses. His voice went squeaky when he was in a panic. 'We don't have time for—'

'Gotta *make* time,' said Mitchell, taking a bite from his sandwich. Golden, wet egg slopped down his chin. He grinned, chewing with his mouth open, then took a swig of tea.

They were a funny pair, Annie thought: both tall, good-looking, but only Mitchell knew it. He wore his dark hair long, he hadn't shaved and there was that bad-boy look in his eyes. Annie thought there was something predatory, thrilling, almost wolfish about him. Which was ironic, Mitchell being a vampire. George was the werewolf.

Well, not right at the moment. For all but one night each month, George Sands was a big, sweet lunk who you wanted to give a hug. He was broader than Mitchell, a bit taller, too, and yet somehow so much more vulnerable.

No, that wasn't quite right. Annie had glimpsed the anger inside George, the frustration and fury not just at being a werewolf but at even the slightest concern. Like with being late for work.

'The new administrator—' George told Mitchell, hopping from foot to foot.

'Would agree,' Mitchell nodded, teasing, 'that this is the most important meal of the day.' He winked rakishly at Annie, who grinned back at him. Mitchell could be *such* a charmer.

George took his tea from Annie.

'Say thank you to Annie,' said Mitchell.

'Thank you to Annie,' sighed George.

Annie patted his arm. 'You're very welcome,' she said, wrapping her grey cardie around herself.

George took another contented sip of his tea, allowing himself to relax.

'Come on,' said Mitchell, slapping him on the

back so he almost spilt the tea. 'Can't be late for the new administrator!'

He blew Annie a kiss, dumped his plate and mug by the sink and, lugging a bag over his shoulder, vanished through the front door.

George fumed for a moment, eyes raised to the ceiling, then followed Mitchell out into the street. Annie followed, stopping on the doorstep, leaning against the frame to wave them off.

The house they shared was on the corner of a tightly packed Victorian terrace, all the buildings painted in sunny, pastel colours. They were at the top of a really steep hill and the parking round Totterdown was terrible. Yet it had a close, community feel to it. Annie herself didn't know many of their neighbours by name. Lurking in the doorway she watched Mitchell say good morning to the little old lady who lived a few houses along. He could charm anyone, even wearing dark glasses in the grey and rain. It wasn't that he made himself appear safe or anything – people were charmed *because* he seemed a bit dangerous.

Annie watched George run to catch up with Mitchell. He said something to Mitchell, head dipped to one side like a loyal dog. They passed the old woman and ducked round the side of the house, down the hill into the city. The vampire and the werewolf, the most unlikely of friends, off to their bog-ordinary jobs.

Leaving the ghost at home, alone.

Annie felt suddenly self-conscious on the doorstep. The old woman was coming up the street towards her, still smiling at whatever Mitchell had said. Annie stepped back quickly into the safety of the house, slamming the door.

She stood there, perfectly still, bare feet feeling cold on the black and white tiles. She looked down at them, her bare feet and the leggings she'd worn ever since she'd fallen down the stairs. The tile just behind her right heel was cracked from where she'd hit her head. The very spot where she'd died.

A chill ran through her. She was alone. Another day with only herself for company, too terrified to go outside in case anyone noticed her. And yet, in here, cocooned in the house, she was still at the mercy of...

To her right, in the living room, the stereo looked back at her from the shelves. The telly was just out of sight round the corner, in the nook under the stairs. They both taunted her. She didn't dare go near anything electrical, not even the toaster. The radio and telly were how *they* spoke to her. The men with sticks and ropes, the dark forces she'd glimpsed when she died. Annie had ignored the doors they had sent her, doors that appeared in a wall or a corner where there wasn't normally a door. Doors that led ghosts through to whatever fate awaited...

Annie had ignored the doors they had sent her, and someone was furious. They'd seethed at her through the radio and telly, whenever she was alone. They'd played her that old song from the war, a message just for her.

'We'll meet again…'

She knew it was just a matter of time. They'd come for her, some time when she was alone. And she was alone all the time.

Annie knew it was there before she even looked round. She felt suddenly, desperately cold. The living said it felt like someone had walked across your grave; they had no idea how right that was.

She could not move, could not turn round, but knew it was there, just behind her. Slowly, with effort, she turned just her head, in the direction of the kitchen.

She couldn't breathe. She couldn't stop herself from staring. At the shape in the shadow of wall. At the door where there shouldn't be a door.

They had come for her.

Chapter
ONE

The sun came out as they headed down Victoria Terrace, the green bump of Victoria Park rising ahead of them, and beyond it the city of Bristol. If anything, the sun made the morning colder, the grey, wintry light sharpening the features of the park and trees.

Yet, Mitchell noticed, George still beamed at the warmth on his face. Mitchell scowled. Sunlight made him itchy, brought him out in a rash. He dug in the pockets of his leather jacket for a cigarette.

George obviously took that to mean something. He stopped, turning to look at Mitchell. Mitchell stopped too, cupping a hand round the end of the cigarette as he lit it, protecting it from the breeze. He inhaled a long lungful of smoke, then exhaled through his nose with a sigh.

'What?' he asked George, who was still watching him, his head cocked on one side, set in one of his 'sympathetic' faces.

'I'm sure it's going to be fine,' George told him.

'Sure,' said Mitchell, shrugging. They started to walk again, Mitchell as ever just in front, George trotting behind. 'New guy running the hospital. Poking about, asking questions. What can possibly go wrong?'

'We don't know what he's here for. It's probably just money. You know, efficiency. Savings.'

'Redundancies,' said Mitchell. 'Ah, come on. That's the bright side?'

'Well, yeah, it's not great,' said George. 'But you know what it's like these days. Redundancies would be normal. And normal's good.'

Mitchell shook his head, laughing. But when he spoke he was perfectly serious. 'We need these jobs, George,' he said. 'We need the hospital.'

George opened his mouth to say something, then reconsidered. He tried to say something else, then considered again. Finally he just said, 'I know.'

They needed the hospital because it kept them normal. They were part of a community, a small part of the mass of humanity. It wasn't glamorous. They were just porters, doing the jobs anyone else could get out of. But it meant they were paying something back, making an act of contrition.

Mitchell had got the idea from a thing in the paper about Alcoholics Anonymous. This guy talked about how difficult it was, living an ordinary life when you were an addict. You felt separate and dirty and self-conscious, adrift from the rest of humanity. Mitchell knew exactly how that felt. So the AA sometimes got new, awkward members to go round after a session and clear up all the ashtrays.

It was a dirty, smelly job. There'd be cigarette butts on the floor, under chairs, and you'd have to dig them out with your fingers. You'd be there on your knees, down in the muck and ash. And you felt, for a moment, normal. Blessedly mundane. A little humility and care for others and you could maybe buy back your soul. Running errands round the hospital gave Mitchell and George that same sense of regaining grace.

But there were other, practical reasons for wanting to stay at the hospital. George needed the old isolation ward down in the bowels of the building, a vault with a sturdy door. Once a month he could lock himself in there. The wolf was free to wreak havoc and no one could get hurt. Mitchell, too, had access to packets and packets of blood, which didn't really work but just about kept him from feasting on anyone walking past. It was the perfect place for them, living among the humans, invisible, and doing no one any harm.

'They won't sack porters,' said George as they crossed the road and followed the pavement running alongside the river. 'They don't pay us enough for it to make a difference.'

Mitchell exhaled a long plume of smoke. He didn't need to say it, but he wasn't just worried about whether they'd keep their jobs.

They kept on in silence, down York Road, the river on their right. The sun glittered on the water in the Avon and in the windows of the gentrified buildings on the bank. Nothing ever stayed the same. Bristol had transformed in the years Mitchell had known it. This smart, pretty marina had once been thick with smoke and activity, ships crowded into every available landing. Bristol had made its fortune in trade – in silks and spices and even human beings. It had been a nexus point, a gateway into Britain, or out to the rest of the world. Which was why the vampires had chosen it.

They had run the city, invisibly, for centuries. There were vampire customs men, dockers and magistrates. They had their own people in the police force, the hospitals and council. A funeral parlour, in the innocuous name of one B. Edwards, acted as their headquarters. So there were never any sightings of vampires, not ones that were taken seriously or even written down. There were no records of bodies found with two telling holes in their necks. Death certificates and police reports always said natural causes, accidents or disease. Whatever the vampires fancied, whatever kept them out of sight.

They'd had the freedom of the city. They could walk where they wanted by night or by day. They were untouchable, like princes.

Until George's wolf killed had Herrick. Then everything had changed.

Oh, George had done it in self-defence – to protect himself and Mitchell and the house. Herrick had tried to start a war. But with the chief vampire gone the system was collapsing. The vampires were coming apart, laying low or fighting among themselves. There was no one to doctor the bodies and forms, no one to hide the city's abnormal death rate. And it was starting to show.

And now the Department of Health had sent this new guy. Was he here to look into it all? Mitchell had even found himself hoping that Dr McGough would be a vampire himself, would help cover up all these questions. But the other vampires had never heard of him.

Dr McGough didn't seem to be a vampire. For a start, there were too many photographs of him on Google.

No, as far as Mitchell could tell he was merely some chinless bureaucrat from Whitehall, with a history of mass sackings and IT projects that didn't work. His PhD, said *Private Eye*, had been in the economics of management. Which meant he used a lot of jargon as he wielded the knife.

Staff at the hospital had of course been told there was nothing to worry about. And the more often they'd been told that, the more their worries grew.

Mitchell and George crossed the old, iron bridge

that was also a roundabout, and cut through the car park to the back entrance of the hospital. Mitchell stubbed out his cigarette and lit another as they followed the grey stone edifice round to the main entrance on Little Guinea Street. Other smokers usually huddled in their scrubs and lab-coats just outside the gate, a vital source of comradeship and gossip. But not today.

There was no one there. There weren't even cigarette butts littering the pavement.

Mitchell glanced at George; he could clearly feel it too. A tension in the air. George checked his watch.

'Ten to,' he told Mitchell. They were still, technically, on time. But Mitchell stamped out the cigarette he'd only just started and they both hurried inside.

The main patients' waiting area was oddly quiet, too. There were patients, filling up the rows of chairs, trying not to sit too close to one another. They stared mutely into space, read magazines or watched the telly high up in the corner. The breakfast news had a story about yet more concerns in the City – meaning London and banks and lost millions. Mitchell had lived through enough stock-market crashes to know the way it went. The bankers got hit first, but the effects slowly spiralled out into the high street. Job losses, cutbacks, the exhaustion in people's faces, the sporadic violence.

A few of the patients looked round as George and Mitchell hurried in. But Mitchell knew better than to meet their eyes as he plucked off his dark glasses. Eye contact gave them permission to approach you. They'd start listing their symptoms and how long they'd been waiting and then you'd be trapped. George and Mitchell bustled on.

Because, bar Sarah, the pretty girl on reception, there was no sign of any hospital staff. No nurses chasing paper, no hectic frisson in the air. Something else was happening, off behind the scenes.

Through the double doors they passed into the bay of cubicles where patients would be treated. The bays were silent – no patients being tended, no doctors doing the tending. They could hear a voice down the corridor, in the mess room. A posh voice, confident, overly sincere.

'... starting down a new road, better engaging your skills and expertise...'

George and Mitchell found the mess room packed with people – doctors, nurses, admin staff, even the cleaners who were just college kids earning minimum wage. All huddled up to hear the man in tailored tweeds, carnation in his lapel.

Mitchell nudged one of the nurses, Kaz – all blonde hair in hippy braids. She gestured back, showing she couldn't move up any more, that there wasn't room. George and Mitchell hovered in the doorway.

Mitchell felt suddenly claustrophobic, the great press of bodies in front of him, hot in the stifling room. He could hear their hearts beating, the blood surging in their veins. His hands began to shake.

Glancing back, he focused on the empty bays, the open space. He bit his lip, determined not to let the bloodlust take him.

'More latecomers,' he heard the man in the tweeds smile benignly.

Mitchell turned, smiling back. A long bead of sweat glistened on the man's temple, just below the terrible comb-over. The hair had been greased into a single, plastic-looking flap, stuck fast to the man's shiny scalp.

Dr Declan McGough spoke with a nasal, public school accent that had probably been beaten into him as a kid. The tweed suit and checked, cotton shirt were soft and tactile fabrics, but they'd seen a lot of starch. His cufflinks glittered at the ends of his sleeves.

'No, not late,' said Dr McGough, wiping at his forehead with a scarlet handkerchief. He made a show of checking his fob watch. 'I should apologise. It's me that's ahead of schedule. By nearly four whole minutes.'

This was, thought Mitchell, a man who had rituals for everything, who'd lecture you on how to make tea or use semi-colons correctly. A man in love with his own background and upbringing, who had nothing of any practical value to offer.

The sort of unmissable parasite Mitchell had once preyed on. Back then, he could almost believe he'd been doing humanity a favour.

Dr McGough snapped the watch shut, returned it to his pocket and smiled radiantly at the hot crowd in front of him. He behaved like a showman, as though they were lapping this up. 'But this is all good,' he said. 'Catching you unawares. In situ, so to speak.'

Mitchell sighed. This guy was a disaster.

McGough must have heard, or seen Mitchell's look of boredom. He now addressed Mitchell directly. 'I was sharing with your colleagues,' he said, a sharpness in his eyes, 'some of what's going to happen. You need to know where we're headed.'

Mitchell swallowed, surprised by the edge in the man's voice. He was aware of George and Kaz, looking round at him. Mitchell had been singled out.

And then McGough was smiling again, and addressing another part of the room. 'I'm not here to test you,' he said warmly. 'I'm here to understand. When I can understand then I can help you. Improve on the excellent work already being done. You all already know what works well. And you know where the gaps are, what can be done better or more efficiently.'

He sighed. 'A horrible word, I know,' he admitted. 'But efficiency means that we all fulfil our potential. That's what I'm here for. We'll talk about goals and targets another time. My first task is just to catch up with you. So carry on as normal and pretend I'm not here.'

He beamed at them, as if the assembly were over. The staff started to turn, to speak to each other. But Dr McGough raised his hand.

'One more thing,' he said sternly. 'I might ask some of you questions. I need you to be honest. Say what you think, not what you think I want to hear. I'm afraid I've no patience for lies.' He let that hang in the air for a moment, then smiled once again. 'And then we can all move forward down the road together...'

The staff waited this time, but Dr McGough had finished. Gradually, colleagues dared whisper to one another, continuing conversations about where they'd been the night before and who else was sharing their shifts. Ignoring as best they could the man who had come into their midst.

'So,' said George, pushing his glasses back up his nose. 'Efficiency. That's all.'

'So,' muttered Mitchell. 'Redundancies.'

Kaz glared at Mitchell, like he'd tempted fate just by saying the word out loud. Yeah, Kaz was just the type to believe in fate. He grinned at her and she glared again, immune to his usual charms. Head too full of wind chimes and dreamcatchers for his tastes anyway, he thought. Soon Kaz was back gossiping with her friends. Mitchell and George stood together, at the back of the assembly. People passed them, returning to work and the ordinary stuff of the day.

'OK,' said George quietly, watching Dr McGough

across the room. Coffee and biscuits had been laid out for anyone wanting to hang around. McGough stood proudly beside a gleaming new coffee machine, the curvaceous design right out of an advert. 'Is he...' George continued as they watched McGough work the controls with a flourish. 'Is he anything we need to worry about?'

No one wanted to have coffee with the new administrator. He poured a few cups himself, tried to hand them out. But those who took the coffee had work to get back to; they took the coffee and left him. They knew he was already watching, Mitchell thought. And perhaps there was something else. Some unconscious, animal instinct warned them that Dr McGough was a danger.

Mitchell inhaled, letting his own predatory instincts take over. He could hear the blood pulsing through the veins of everyone still in the room. He could single them out, the fit, young ones, the ones ground down by long hours and smoking, a guy in the corner still a bit drunk from the night before.

And Dr McGough, heart beating with irritation, a fussy little man. Not vampire, not werewolf, not anything special. Just an ordinary man.

'Nothing to worry about,' Mitchell told George as he opened his eyes.

And he found Dr McGough gazing back at him from across the room. Holding his eye for a moment, a beat, then moving on to offer the nurses his coffee.

But Mitchell kept gazing at him, mouth open in surprise. The look McGough had given him, the look Mitchell knew only too well. The look of a hunter, a predator, scrutinising prey.

Chapter
Two

'He looked at you, *right* at you,' George said to Mitchell as they left the locker room, now dressed in their pale blue scrubs.

'Yeah,' said Mitchell. 'Probably read that in a book on management technique. Make eye contact with everyone you can. Make them feel you're addressing them directly. Come on, that was getting old in the '80s.'

'You know there's something weird about him,' George insisted.

'OK,' said Mitchell. 'He's weird. Sure. Like a headmaster or something.'

'So what are we going to do?'

Mitchell considered. 'Nothing.'

'Nothing?' George almost shouted the word, and must have realised it from Mitchell's own reaction.

He looked quickly round. A couple of nurses looked back at them from the end of the corridor. George waved at them, irritably. 'Yes, hello?' The two nurses scowled.

'Nothing that draws any attention,' said Mitchell, taking George's arm and pulling him away. 'You heard what the man said. We carry on as normal.'

George's whole body sagged as he let himself be led off. 'All right,' he said.

'But keep your eyes open,' said Mitchell.

'And my ears,' nodded George. 'And my —'

'Yeah, OK,' Mitchell told him. 'We'll compare notes at lunch.'

The rest of the day passed in a blur. There was always a job for a spare porter, so they were never spare. Patients had to be ferried to the wards or to X-ray. Bloods and other bits from people had to be taken for testing, and then the results collected. Sometimes equipment needed fetching, usually when it was heavy.

Mitchell liked the bustle of his job. It meant the shift zipped along and he didn't get bored, and it stopped him getting down. There were posters in some of the treatment rooms with advice for recovering addicts. The trick, they said, to keeping clean was simply to keep busy. Yeah, if Mitchell was going to keep off the blood, he depended on activity.

That said, even on the busiest shifts there were

occasional pauses. There'd be the odd cigarette break or chance encounter with a mate. He'd stop to swap gossip, the lifeblood of the building. Who fancied who, who was breaking up, who would get promotion, who was *such a bitch*... Mitchell liked the minutiae of other people's lives, the details of ordinary, tangled existence.

But not today. The staff weren't just on their best behaviour, they were all running in fear.

Mitchell shook his head wearily as he watched the timid creatures scurrying about. Doctors usually stuck to an unofficial rule, only running in the hospital when called to a cardiac arrest. This morning, though, they all hurried from ward to ward, some of them jogging past Mitchell as he made his rounds. Their cheeks burnt pink and their hearts hammered with exertion – if only Mitchell could hear them. Sensible, experienced practitioners, gone to pieces the moment their tenures were threatened. Mitchell found it getting to him. As a predator, he thrived on the panic of the crowd.

And then he got sent down to the refrigerated stores in the basement of the hospital. One of the patients in Lucas Unit needed more blood on hand. Mitchell had a legitimate reason to be helping himself to the stuff. He had never been stopped before. Yet as he stepped into the vault, shelves hidden in fog and icicles, all his instincts screamed aloud that he was being watched.

He glanced round, ducking his head out the door

and back up the corridor. Then he flinched, wincing at his own stupidity – how could he look any more guilty?

There was no one around, no one he could see. He knew he was being foolish, scaring himself. Imagine, a vampire being frightened by shadows.

Even so, he waited, listening, just to be on the safe side. He could see nothing, hear nothing but his own ragged breath. No, he was down here alone. And Mitchell wouldn't show up on any cameras.

Perhaps that was what he could sense, them watching on CCTV, ready to expose the invisible man rifling through the fridges. Had they spotted that blood had gone missing before? Had they set him a trap?

He stepped back into the vault, taking his time, struggling to make it look casual. There didn't seem to be any cameras anywhere, but he didn't want to look too carefully. No, all he could do was complete the task he'd been set. Fetch the blood, take it back up to the ward, then take whatever came.

His hands trembled as he opened a door and looked in on the packets of scarlet liquid, radiant in the light of the fridge. They would know how this stuff made him feel, how inadequate it was compared to a fresh vein and yet how much he depended on it. They could read his thoughts in every move he made.

He carried the blood up to Lucas Unit, the whole time feeling their eyes on him. No one stopped him, but he felt them watching, biding their time. That was the terror inside him – the terror inside them all. They all felt exposed and vulnerable. They all waited for the axe to drop.

The patients picked up on the climate of fear as well. The old dears didn't chatter to Mitchell as he wheeled them to and from their various tests. They sat slumped in their wheelchairs, dead weights. Mitchell didn't mention the old film stars and singers that another day might have sprung them from the stupor of sickness. He didn't do anything that might draw more attention.

Dr McGough himself would be glimpsed, stalking the corridors and wards as if he were just out for a stroll. Mitchell knew better, could see him prowling for the weak ones in the herd, the ones he could pick off most easily. He pretended not to notice the new administrator, what with being so caught up in his work.

Mitchell didn't stop to meet George for lunch. No one seemed to be taking their lunch breaks. The trolley that came round the wards mid-afternoon hardly sold any tea. They pressed on, working every moment, desperate not to give the new administrator reason to strike them down.

The pretence took its toll as the afternoon wore on. Staff looked exhausted by four o'clock, eyes red and raw from the relentless effort.

Mitchell was on a ward when it broke. A junior doctor, a guy new enough to the hospital that

Mitchell hadn't yet learned his name, dropped a file of papers. The file hit the plastic floor with a *thwap*. Heads turned all down the ward in time to see the file burst apart, scattering pages all around.

The junior doctor, horrified, quickly knelt down to gather up the pages. Mitchell could see that a couple of pages had slipped under the bed of one of the patients. He did not go to help. The staff were all too busy to notice what had happened. That's what they all pretended, Mitchell like everyone else.

Because they'd seen Dr McGough on the ward as well. He made his way calmly over to the hapless junior doctor, still on his knees. Dr McGough smiled benignly as he picked up one, scattered page and handed it to the doctor.

'Patient information is priceless,' he chided, smoothing his ridiculous comb-over with the flat of one hand. 'We treat it with as much care as if it were about ourselves. I'm sure you've been trained in data protection.'

The doctor said nothing, just nodded, knowing he'd just been marked down. He and Dr McGough gathered the rest of the pages, and then Dr McGough left him alone, heading off to inspect somewhere else. The hapless doctor slunk off too, away from the colleagues who had left him to his fate.

Mitchell felt wretched – he should have done something. But he also felt a huge sense of relief. It was as if everyone in the hospital could let out the breath they'd all been holding. The administrator had claimed his first victim and it had been someone else.

Finally the ordeal was over. Mitchell worked a bit over the end of his shift in case he was being observed. Then he made his way back to the lockers and gratefully stripped out of his scrubs.

Shedding the light blue uniform seemed to shed a lot of the weight of the day. In his long-sleeved T-shirt and boxers he was just a civilian, not someone caught up in the terrible game. His shoulders ached from where he'd been so tense.

He pulled on his jeans and leather jacket, and made his way out into the night. As soon as he got off the hospital premises he lit a much-needed cigarette, his first since the start of the day. Smoke filled his lungs and he felt the nicotine ignite his cold, vampire blood.

Perhaps it didn't really have any effect on him; it was the ritual of lighting up and inhaling that brought him comfort. He didn't mind, either way. Rituals could be important. Look at Annie, making endless cups of tea that she couldn't drink.

'Bad day?' asked George.

Mitchell didn't flinch. George had been hiding just out of the light of the street lamp, but Mitchell had seen him straight away.

'Not the best,' said Mitchell. 'You?'

'They've gone mad!' said George. 'The nurses ask you to get something then snap at you for getting it.

And Mr Saunders called me a wimp!'

'Laurie Saunders can talk.' Using their first names was an old trick; it made the surgeons that much less grand. Almost made them human.

'We've all been running scared,' said George.

'Normal day for you, then,' grinned Mitchell.

George scowled at him. 'Don't say you didn't feel it as well.'

Mitchell took another long drag of his cigarette. 'All right. There's been something in the air all day. Something unnatural.'

'More than just management technique?'

'Maybe,' said Mitchell. 'Come on.'

They began the long trek home, crossing the iron bridge then following the road left, alongside the river. George began to plan the rest of their evening: what food they had in, what he could cook with it, what wine they should get on the way. As they made their way up the steep slope of Windsor Terrace, they were arguing about DVDs.

They reached the top of the hill and the pink house on the corner where they lived. George fussed around, finding his key. Mitchell stood on the pavement waiting, looking up and down their street. There was no one else out in the darkness. Light peeked warmly from behind the drawn curtains and blinds in some windows. Mitchell smiled. He loved where they lived.

'Um,' he heard George say. He turned quickly.

George had got the front door open. He was

staring into the darkness inside. They could both sense it: something was terribly wrong.

They hurried forward into the house. Mitchell snapped the switch and the lights glared bright. It took a split second for his eyes to adjust. He'd been expecting carnage, or some weird poltergeist stuff. But no, there was Annie, sat at the foot of the stairs.

She looked awful. Her hands were shaking, and she didn't even look up at them.

'Wh-what's happened?' asked George, running over to her.

Annie just raised her hand, in the direction of the kitchen. At the door in the wall where there shouldn't have been a door.

'They've come for you,' said Mitchell. 'Annie, if it's time, you have to go through.'

'No!' said George. 'We discussed this. Annie stays if she wants to.'

'Annie,' said Mitchell sternly. 'You know that's why it's here.'

Annie looked up at him, her eyes wild with fear and fury. 'Oh yeah?' she said. 'You know all about it, do you?'

'Annie,' said Mitchell more softly. 'Why else would it be here?'

Annie smiled at him, viciously. 'Ask *her*. She came through it.'

George and Mitchell both turned where Annie nodded, to look into the living room.

At the woman sat on the sofa.

Chapter
THREE

She sat perfectly still, staring at the fireplace, ignoring the three housemates watching her. George took a step forward to confront her, but Mitchell held him back. They continued to stare at the visitor.

She was a tall, statuesque black woman in late middle age. Her big, purple hat perched on painstakingly lacquered hair, her big purple coat concealed a floral dress in brilliant colours. George thought she looked dressed up for church or some other special occasion. Ghosts usually wore the clothes that they'd died in. But this woman had made more of an effort.

He could tell just from looking that she was a ghost. Perhaps it helped that he'd lived with Annie so long. Or it was the whiff she gave off, something dark and industrial not quite within his conscious perception but that made his nostrils itch. Being a werewolf gave George heightened senses, but he couldn't always explain the sensations themselves. This woman had an aroma like dark magic. He thought it might be brimstone, not that he'd smelled that before.

She sat there, inscrutably, staring forward. Like *they* were the intruders.

George turned to Mitchell. 'Who is she?' he whispered. 'This is our house!'

'I know,' said Mitchell. He turned to Annie. 'Has she said anything? Do we know her name?'

Annie looked terrified as she shook her head. 'I didn't ask.' It must be worse for her, thought George. Another ghost poaching on her territory.

'OK,' George told her. 'It's going to be OK.'

Annie looked up at him and forced herself to smile. George felt emboldened just from the look on her face. He'd always felt protective of Annie.

He stepped forward into the living room, towards the woman on the sofa. She did not look round.

'Er,' he said. 'Now I'm sure you think you've got a very good reason to be here. But this is our house, and we don't know who you are.'

She turned her head slowly, looking up at him, appraising him. Her eyes met his and he took a step backwards. She stared at him from some infinite distance, such pain and loss within her.

'Er,' said George. 'Hello. Hi. I'm, um, George. Can you tell us your name?'

The woman stared at him with dark and fathomless eyes, wells of despair drawing him in. Then a thought seemed to strike her. Her brow furrowed as she tried to drag the long-forgotten memory back into the light.

'Jeh,' she said. Something sparked in her eyes. Her mouth twitched into the first hint of a smile. 'Gemma,' she said. 'My name was Gemma Romain.'

Annie made tea. Not for herself or the ghost who had imposed herself on them – ghosts didn't eat or drink. But Mitchell and George could both do with a brew, and it kept her out in the kitchen. Away from the woman and the door. She cringed as she listened to George and Mitchell fussing around the woman, teasing out who she'd once been. Every word this Gemma spoke was like an icy touch to Annie. For the first time since she had died, Annie felt her skin prickle with goose bumps.

'It must have been the end of September 1999,' the woman explained as Annie brought in the two mugs of tea. George sat beside Gemma on the low, leather sofa, Mitchell stood on the far side of the coffee table. Annie hovered just behind him. For all she looked immaculate in her hat and coat, the woman didn't half stink. There was something acrid about her, like out of a chemistry lab at school. Annie could taste it at the back of her throat.

She hoped it wasn't a ghost thing, that she didn't smell like that herself. But no, Gilbert hadn't smelled like this. A bit of BO but not this acrid, industrial tang.

'I had cancer in my bones,' the woman continued.

Annie flinched. Maybe she could smell chemotherapy or some other heavy treatment. She glanced at Mitchell, then at George, but they didn't seem to notice the smell.

'And there was also...' The woman tailed off, staring at the floor.

Oh, get on with it, thought Annie.

'Go on,' said Mitchell, more kindly.

The woman nodded, not looking back up at him. 'I had pills for my angina. I think it was my heart that did me. But I can't remember the moment. I mean, not how it felt.'

'Memory can be funny that way,' George told her. 'You'd think something as big as that would stick in your mind for a bit. But we don't always remember pain. It's like we're spared it, or it's how we survive.'

'And if it was your heart,' said Mitchell, 'it probably would have been quick. It's a good way to go.'

The woman nodded. Mitchell sipped his tea. No one said anything. They all felt awkward, making small talk with this woman about the way she'd died. Like they pussy-footed around the subject of Owen, Annie's ex-fiancée and their landlord. Gemma just sat there, straight-backed and serious, answering their questions.

Annie remembered how awful it had been when she'd come back herself. The confusion, the fear, the straight refusal to believe what had happened to her. How could this woman be so deathly calm about it? And why did the boys have to be considerate and reasonable? She wanted to scream at them: this woman shouldn't be here! They should just shove her back through the door she had come in by.

Annie couldn't stand it any longer. 'Ask her why she's here.'

Mitchell glanced at her, surprised. '*She* has got a name,' he told her.

'I just mean,' said Annie, squirming from his gaze. 'People don't normally come *back* through a door. Do they?'

'She's right,' said George. 'Gemma. Do you know what you're here for?'

Gemma gazed up at him forlornly, eyes wide. 'I don't know where this is.'

'It's my house,' Annie told her. 'I'm the one who died here.'

'Annie,' said Mitchell. 'She needs our help.'

'Is that why I'm here?' asked Gemma.

'This building used to be a pub,' George told Gemma. 'It might have been a pub when you were alive. Maybe that's it: you used to come here. We know it was called the Corner House. Because it's on the corner.' He pointed at the window above their front door, the words 'Corner House' backwards in the frosted glass, facing the street outside.

Gemma shook her head, sniffed. 'I don't go to any pubs.'

'What's wrong with pubs?' asked Annie. 'I worked in a—'

'You're in Totterdown,' said Mitchell. 'In Bristol. Do you know where that is?'

Gemma nodded. 'I know Bristol. I live in St George's.'

'But that's the other side of town,' said George.

'Can you think of any reason that would bring you here?' asked Mitchell. 'Someone you knew or something that happened. Something with unfinished business.'

Gemma slowly nodded, to herself. 'Totterdown was up on the hill,' she said. 'All those pretty, coloured houses.'

'Yes,' said Mitchell. 'That's us. You remember! So what were you doing here? Why've you come back?'

Gemma smiled at him sadly. 'I never went to Totterdown. Never. I just saw it, up on the hill.'

George and Mitchell exchanged glances. 'Then why?' asked George.

'It must be us,' said Mitchell. 'We're here. We can help her. We helped Annie find out why she hadn't moved on.'

'Yeah,' said Annie caustically. 'And that really worked out great.'

But a thought had struck Annie, one that chilled her to the bone. She took a step forward.

'Did they send you here because of me?' said Annie. 'Have you brought a message?'

Gemma sat thinking, struggling to recall the memories.

'Who's *they*?' asked George. Mitchell motioned to him to be quiet.

Gemma looked up at Annie, her eyes wide with fear. She clearly knew who Annie meant.

'There wasn't a message,' she said. 'I don't know why I'm here. I keep seeing…' She tailed off, still holding Annie's gaze. A tear squeezed from her eye and trickled down her cheek. 'I don't know what the rope means.'

Annie stared back, emotions whirling inside her. This woman had seen what she'd seen, on the other side of the door. The dark powers who commanded the dead. Gemma was just as much at their mercy as Annie.

'It's all right,' Annie found herself saying. 'We'll work it out.' They were refugees from that malevolent place. They had to stick together.

Gemma continued to stare at her. And then her face lit up and she smiled a radiant smile, her eyes bright with tears. 'Thank you,' she said, almost without making any sound. 'Thank you.' Annie grinned back. Mitchell was grinning too.

Annie turned to George, but he was looking off in the direction of the kitchen. He turned back, a concerned expression on his face.

'What?' said Annie.

'The door,' he told her. 'The door she came through. It's gone.'

George cooked a fantastic pasta. Annie, Mitchell and Gemma sat at the small table in the kitchen to enjoy the performance. George explained as he chopped that the peppers were from the organic shop where the women behind the counter all knew him. The tight ringlets of green and orange pasta were trottole tricolore, made from durum wheat. George liked, he said, to let them sit in the boiling water for ages, so they got super-soft. They were also perfect, he boasted, with his homemade meatballs.

'George,' Mitchell told Gemma, 'has amazing balls.'

Gemma exploded. Her laughter shook the whole kitchen, and made Mitchell spill his wine. As the housemates watched, the woman rocked in her seat, holding her sides. 'Balls,' she wheezed with delighted. 'His balls!'

'*Meat*balls,' George tried to explain, but that only made Gemma laugh all the harder.

Mitchell rolled his eyes and poured himself another glass of ruby-coloured wine.

George served up, ladling great steaming chunks of pasta and veg into two bowls. Mitchell had laid four places, so the women didn't feel left out. He and George tucked in, ravenous after a long day's work. Annie kept the conversation going as they chewed. She told Gemma about the films Mitchell made them watch, how much she preferred Buster Keaton to Harold Lloyd. Mitchell, mouth full, tried to cut across her. Gemma interrupted, saying she'd always liked Laurel and Hardy.

Mitchell clapped his hands together. 'Right,' he declared. 'That settles it.'

'Oh no,' said George, rolling his eyes. 'Gemma, you've set him off.'

After George and Mitchell had eaten, Mitchell led them through to the living room to watch *Babes in Toyland*. Annie had to concede that, all right, it wasn't so bad. George worried it was a bit fascist in places, but no else saw the march of wooden toys as sinister. And anyway, it had been made years before the war. Mitchell kept telling them when good bits were coming, and towards the end he couldn't keep quiet about all the things the film was referencing.

Annie watched Gemma. She watched the film and she watched George and Mitchell, smiling indulgently while they bickered with each other. Gemma seemed happy – and not at all fazed that Mitchell had been around in the 1930s. It was no stranger than dying in 1999 and coming back a decade later. Annie liked that Gemma was coping, accepting this strange new existence. She seemed to be coping better than Annie ever had.

When the film finished, they caught the end of the news. Gemma drank in the details of the recession and her enthusiasm began to work on Annie, too. Annie had ignored the news even when she'd been alive; now she found herself drawn to the complex arguments involved. Companies blamed the government for letting them go bankrupt, the government blamed the companies' greed. Millions of people were going to lose their jobs and were angry, bewildered, resigned. There were going to be cuts to the public sector, which meant teachers and doctors being out of work.

'Oh,' said Annie to George and Mitchell. 'You're worried about your jobs!' They all looked round at her, surprised. 'What?' she said. 'OK, I only just worked that out.'

Mitchell got to his feet. 'Work in the morning,' he told them and loped off to bed without even saying goodnight.

'Have I said something stupid?' asked Annie. She grinned at Gemma. 'I always do that.'

'I'm sure you don't,' Gemma told her, which made Annie feel all warm inside.

Yeah, maybe Gemma was good news.

'They're watching us at work,' George explained. 'Say they need to make some savings. You know. They're not saying redundancies but everyone knows what they mean. So we're all a bit on edge.'

'Yeah,' said Annie. 'But you two are safe.' George didn't answer her. 'Aren't you?'

'Hope so,' said George. 'Won't be much use at anything else.' He took a sip from the glass of wine that he'd finished an hour before. Annie let the matter drop.

They idly watched the late film on BBC One –
something about a kidnapped girl, though none of
them were really paying attention. Annie wanted to
tell George that things would be OK or give him
a hug, but she couldn't with Gemma sat between
them. George twitched under Annie's gaze. When
he looked round at her all she could do was shrug
and smile at him, which just put him even less at
ease. She could see he wanted to escape, but couldn't
allow himself to be so rude when they had a guest.
George was working a later shift than Mitchell, so
going up to bed now might be construed as a snub.
For all his frustration and inner turmoil, George
had immaculate manners. Annie was desperate to
help him relax.

'I could make you a hot chocolate,' she said,
suddenly leaping to her feet.

'Uh, yeah OK,' said George, too polite to say no.

'I can make it,' said Gemma, getting to her feet as
well. She and Annie appraised each other.

'It's all right,' said Annie. 'I can manage.'

Gemma lowered her head. 'But you've all been so
kind to me. I want to do something.'

Annie felt awful – she'd not meant to dismiss
Gemma so easily. She looked to George, who
nodded. Yes, of course Gemma should be able to
pay her way. No one wanted her to be – or feel like
– a burden.

'OK,' said Annie in a small voice. 'Sure.' And yet
as she sat back down, Annie also felt stung. The

chocolate had been her idea, to make George feel better. Gemma had come between them.

Gemma's mouth fell open in concern. 'I don't want to be getting in your way,' she said.

'No,' said Annie. 'No, of course not. It's in a jar in the cupboard on the left.'

Gemma bustled through to the kitchen. George joined Annie on the sofa, moving the cushions around behind him on the throw so that he could get comfy. They listened to the clattering as Gemma found a clean saucepan.

'She seems better,' George whispered to Annie.

'She's OK,' said Annie, still smarting.

'We should keep an eye on her.'

'What do you think she's here for?' asked Annie.

'That's what we're meant to find out.'

'How?' said Annie.

George considered. Then he smiled his nervous smile, his head cocked on one side. 'You'll think of something.'

Mitchell dreamt of eyes, watching him. He knelt by the fridge in the hospital vault, the packets of blood glowing in the light of the open door. The packets weren't easy to open with his teeth, and blood dripped down his chin.

Mitchell loved the feel of blood dripping from his chin.

And the eyes watched him, balefully from the darkness. He knew they were there, but when he turned to look they had vanished. A ghost watching him feast, knowing all his secrets.

He mumbled to himself, turned over in the bed, and dreamt of being watched somewhere else.

The boys slept and, as usual, Annie didn't. She and Gemma spent the rest of the night in the living room. Annie sat with her legs curled underneath her on the sofa, flicking idly through the pages of a magazine. Gemma sat in the corner, perfectly poised, her hands on her lap, saying nothing. Every time Annie looked up, Gemma remained perfectly still. But Annie couldn't shake the sense that she was being watched.

'I don't know how you do it,' Gemma said, breaking the silence. 'Just waiting.'

'You get used to it,' said Annie.

Gemma nodded. She looked like she wanted to say something.

'What?' said Annie.

'I wanted to know,' said Gemma, 'how you died.'

So Annie told her about Owen, and the stairs and the broken tile. She didn't want to say more – that Owen had pushed her, that she'd come back to the house so she could wreak her revenge. And yet Gemma drew it from her, piece by piece.

At about six, with the pink of dawn glowing through the windows and warming the cool, blue room, they sat curled on the sofa together, Annie's head on Gemma's shoulder, tears streaming down her face. She felt like she'd cried her whole life out, drained and yet purified.

She wiped her eyes on her sleeve, sat up to get her breath. Beside her, Gemma seemed as radiant as the dawn, as if the new day had brought her new power. Yet there was something about her eyes that Annie found unsettling. Gemma stared across the room, her expression stern.

'Are you all right?' Annie asked.

'Think so,' said Gemma, not looking round at her. She continued to stare.

'You look,' said Annie, 'haunted.' They both smiled at the word.

'Yes,' said Gemma. She considered. In a low, reverent voice she said, 'You seen it, too.'

Annie sat up straight. 'Seen what?'

'The other side of the door.' Gemma shuddered, almost too scared to say the words. 'The sticks and rope.'

Annie nodded, feeling the stiffness in her neck.

Gemma watched her react, recognised her fear. She glanced back at the shadow she'd been watching. There was a terrible look in her eyes, as if she could see something there on the floorboards before her.

'I don't know why I'm here or what they want,' she told Annie.

Annie looked at the spot on the rug where Gemma was looking. She could only see the rug.

'What is it?' she asked.

Gemma looked back up at her, with what might

have been an awkward smile but could have been a wince.

'I see it in the shadows, when I turn my head.'

Annie swallowed hard. 'What do you see?'

Gemma hesitated. Then she looked right at Annie, her eyes dark and awful to behold. 'I see rope.'

Chapter
FOUR

George struggled to find the alarm clock clattering inside his head. It juddered on the floor by his bed and he knocked it over before he reached it. Then he found his glasses and could read the time.

Ten a.m., with at least 20 minutes before he really needed to get up. He lay on his back, under the duvet, gathering his thoughts. Oh yes, they had a visitor. He should probably get up, see what was happening. Heaving himself out of bed George staggered off to the bathroom.

Annie found him while he was in the shower. He screamed when he saw her there, watching through the curtain. She grinned at him and held up the mug of tea she had made. Gibbering, not able to find the words to express exactly what he thought, George gestured at the shelf for their toothbrushes.

Annie put the mug there. Then she hovered about, grinning awkwardly.

'I,' George told her with epic restraint, 'am in the shower.'

'I can see that,' said Annie, grinning. 'I'll wait.'

He gestured at her, as if shoving her out with his forehead. She grinned, raised one finger and pointed to the bathroom door. 'I'll…' she began, and hurried out.

Sighing, George ducked his head under the spray of hot water. Annie, some instinct told him, needed to speak to him.

'It's not that I don't like her,' Annie whispered as George struggled into his clothes. He'd put some socks on one side, hadn't he? He looked all round, on the dresser, on the bed. But the socks had disappeared.

He turned to Annie. She handed him the socks. George seethed. 'Thank you.'

'She's just weird,' said Annie. 'She just sat there, all night, *watching*.'

'That's what you do,' George told her, putting on his shoes.

'Yeah,' agreed Annie. 'Oh, you mean it should be all right for her to do the same. George! It's my house.' She paused, and George saw her steeling herself to explain what really bothered her. 'She's terrified of something,' she said.

'Terrified of what?' said George.

Annie shrugged quickly. 'I don't know. I'm just saying. Maybe you could talk to her about it.'

George considered. He had his own worries to worry about. 'Did you speak to Mitchell?' he asked.

'He was in a hurry. Said I should speak to you.'

'Thank you, Mitchell.'

'George, what are we going to do?'

George sighed. 'Annie, I've got to go to work.'

'You can't leave me with her!' She immediately slapped her hands over her mouth. Annie had cried that out, loud enough for anyone else in the house to hear.

George waited for Annie to calm down. Her eyes were wide with fear. They both listened for the tread of Gemma's footsteps. Nothing.

'What are you afraid of?' George whispered.

Annie took a deep breath, like she had a whole story to tell him.

Something had got into Annie in the last few days, even before Gemma turned up. She'd been more spooked than usual. George had seen her almost jump out of her skin when he'd turned on the telly. She wouldn't watch it on her own. If either George or Mitchell got up from watching something she would follow them. Which was odd enough when they just went into the kitchen for a drink and worse when they went for a pee.

But whatever it might have been, Annie thought better of telling him. 'She says she sees things.'

'What things?' said George.

'And there's this smell about her.'

'Like chemicals,' said George. 'Like when you strike a match.'

'You smell it too!' grinned Annie. 'You didn't say anything last night.'

George pushed his glasses back up his nose with a finger. 'I'm too well brought up,' he said.

'It's not your fault,' she told him.

'Annie, what do you want me to do?'

Annie folded her arms. Then she unfolded them again, and teased a lock of dark ringlets at her fringe.

'I don't know,' she said. 'It's just… Whatever she's seeing, it can't be good. And she could have brought it with her. It could be in the house.'

'She hasn't got anywhere else,' said George, kindly. 'Nowhere anyone could help her.'

'No,' admitted Annie. She cocked her head, thinking it over. 'She has to stay,' she decided. 'But maybe you could just talk to her.'

George sighed. Anything for an easy life. 'All right,' he said. 'All right.'

'It's not that I don't like her,' said Gemma when George confronted her in the kitchen.

'No, of course,' he told Gemma, trying to hide his impatience. He should really have left for work by now. What with the new administrator and everything, he'd wanted to be in early.

'She goes in your rooms when you're sleeping,' said Gemma. She was a tall, broad woman and George felt intimidated just being in the kitchen beside her. Again, he couldn't help notice the stink around her. A rich, industrial stink he couldn't place but so like striking matches...

'She can go where she wants,' said George. 'It's her house.'

'Not if she's dead,' smiled Gemma. And George thought she might be sulking.

'What's she done to you?' he asked simply.

Gemma considered, then she shrugged her great shoulders, rippling the floral dress all the way down. 'Nothing,' she said. 'I want to help her. She told me about Owen and how she died. She must regret doing that now. Been cold to me ever since.'

'Right,' said George. 'Well, these things take time. And I've got to get to work...'

Gemma stared at him. 'But you haven't drunk your tea!'

He rubbed at his eye with his finger, digging it in behind the lens of his glasses. 'I did. I had the tea Annie made me.'

Gemma pouted. 'But I made you one as well.' She held up the mug.

'Oh,' said George. 'Sorry. Of course.'

He took the tea from her. It had gone cold and she'd put in too much milk. But the way she gazed up at him left him little choice. He took a long sip, forced himself to swallow it, then handed the mug

55

back to her. She beamed. He could have sunned himself in that smile.

'Thank you,' he said. 'But I really have to go. You're both going to be cooped up here until Mitchell gets back. So you're going to have to get along.'

'Of course we'll get on!' laughed Gemma loudly. 'We're both grown-ups.' She chuckled, her whole body shaking at the thought of her and Annie scrapping. 'Boy,' she said eventually, wiping a tear from her eye. 'You've got some funny ideas.'

'But you said,' said George, perplexed now. 'So what's the problem?'

'No problem,' said Gemma, lowering her voice and glancing over her shoulder to ensure Annie didn't overhear. 'Just she doesn't go out, and nobody comes to see her. She's all on her own.'

'She's got me and Mitchell,' said George.

'Yeah, well,' said Gemma, the distaste evident on her face. 'And neither of you's exactly normal.'

'Now hold on,' George began.

'I don't mean any offence,' said Gemma, chucking him on the arm. 'It's just a girl needs a bit of normality, you get what I'm saying? Specially with the state she's in. Needs some looking after.'

'We look after her,' George insisted.

'An' I'm sure you do the best you can,' said Gemma. 'Considering.'

'Considering what?'

'Well,' said Gemma. 'You're boys, aren't you? Cook and clean – in your own fashion. But you can't run a house. Got your work to go to.'

'Yeah,' said George, checking his watch. 'And I—'

'Oh yeah,' declared Gemma, swatting him with both hands, ushering him out of the kitchen to the front door. 'You get to your work.'

'Mitchell will be back by fourish,' said George. 'If he doesn't get waylaid.'

'You're lucky I'm here,' said Gemma, helping George into his coat. 'You know something's bothering that girl. You know she won't share it with you two.'

George looked down at her, arms out in acceptance as she did up his zip. She reached the top and gazed up at him with another radiant smile.

'You'll look after her?' said George.

'Course!'

'Well,' said George. 'That's all right, then. I'm glad you're here, Gemma.'

He turned to go, and stopped. He turned back. Annie sat halfway up the stairs, watching him and Gemma. She'd not been there just a moment before.

'I'm...' said George. 'I guess I'm off now.'

'Yeah,' said Annie quietly, not meeting his eye. She chewed on the fingernail of one thumb, her silver cardigan wrapped tightly around her.

'Mitchell will be back around fourish,' George told her, feeling stupid and clumsy. Gemma was right. *Of course* he could see something was wrong with Annie. But he didn't have time to go into it. 'You'll be all right, won't you?'

'Yeah,' said Annie, still not looking up. 'You go.'

He sighed, turning to the door that Gemma was holding open for him. She smiled at him as he passed her, out into the street. George took a deep breath of the cool, grey day, glad to be out of the house. Then he started down the road to the corner, and the hill down into town.

'George!'

He turned, on the corner, to find Annie racing after him, hair and cardigan streaming behind her. She ran so fast she almost smashed into him, but skidded to a stop just in time.

'What have I forgotten?' asked George. 'You've not made me another packed lunch?'

'No,' said Annie, linking her arm in George's and leading him down the steep hill of Windsor Terrace. 'Come on, I'll walk with you a bit. Keep you company.'

They were buffeted by a morning breeze and occasional flecks of rain. Annie shivered, though George wasn't sure she could really feel the cold. They nodded at Mrs Morgan coming up the hill towards them. George wondered if Mrs Morgan could see him with Annie, or would think he just had his arm sticking out as he walked along. Their neighbours had come to accept that he and Mitchell just behaved a bit strangely. Mitchell said it was good that they didn't judge.

'You really don't like Gemma,' said George to Annie once they were safely out of earshot of Mrs Morgan. 'Look at you. All outside and everything.'

Annie held on to him all the more tightly. 'It's not her I don't like. I feel stupid for telling her my whole life story last night, and crying on her shoulder.'

'Ah,' said George. 'Well, it's probably better she knows.'

'It's not just that, though,' said Annie. 'There's something she's afraid of.'

'What?'

Annie bit her lip, and he could see she wouldn't tell him what she knew – or at least suspected.

'All right,' said George kindly. 'If she's afraid of it, you should be wary, too.'

Annie nodded, hugging George close for being so understanding. She smiled that girlish smile he could never resist.

'But you can't spend all day at work with me,' he told her.

Annie's smile melted away. 'I can't spend all day alone with her,' she pleaded. 'What if the thing she's afraid of comes back?'

'So what are you going to do?'

Annie raised her head from his arm. 'I'll go to the park,' she said, nodding at the hump of green grass and trees on the rise ahead of them.

'It's raining,' said George.

'I don't mind,' said Annie. George had to admit that she didn't look wet at all. Things were a lot easier, he thought, for a ghost. You didn't get steamed-up glasses when you came in from the rain. And you didn't need locking up once a month.

'And what will you do in the park all day?' he asked her. 'You don't like being out on your own.'

Annie bit her lip as she considered.

'She won't be on her own.'

George yelped. Annie had dug her fingernails into his upper arm. She stood frozen to the spot, eyes tightly closed. George turned and Annie had to turn with him. Hurrying down the hill towards them came Gemma, resplendent in her coat and hat. The stout heels on her shoes clip-clopped on the pavement as she came. A woman on a mission.

'Hi,' said George. 'Annie was just—'

'Rushing out without a coat on,' Gemma chided.

'I don't feel the rain,' Annie told her.

'You'll catch your death,' said Gemma. Then she stopped. 'Oh!' she said. 'Oh!' And she started to laugh.

George stared in amazement at the statuesque woman, laughing loudly in the street. She had to bend over, gripping her sides and then one of the low walls of one of the terraced houses. George glanced quickly round, worried someone might see. He didn't handle embarrassment well. A woman and a toddler were making their way up the hill towards them but they didn't look up. George turned to Annie; she didn't seem to know what to do either.

'Oh!' Gemma squeaked. 'Oh! That hurts!' She stood up straight, pressing her fists into her lower spine. 'Oh,' she said, rasping to get her breath back. 'All right,' she said. 'All right, enough.'

'It takes a bit of getting used to,' said Annie.

'Yeah,' sighed Gemma, smiling. 'It's another world.'

'A lot's happened in the last ten years,' said George, eager to be getting on to work. 'It's still the same place really. Just better mobile phones.'

'No,' said Gemma, the smile falling from her face. 'I mean... I haven't laughed in such a long time. Forgotten what it felt like.'

'Ten years,' said Annie and she shivered. 'Dead and in the darkness.'

George put his arm around her but she shrugged him off. He saw the way she now watched Gemma, her expression fixed and serious. The thought of that darkness, of whatever waited in the realm beyond the living, transfixed her. She took a step forwards, up the hill towards Gemma.

'Even before,' said Gemma, recoiling slightly. 'Even before I died, there wasn't that much laughing.'

They stood there, in the cold drizzle, George the only one getting wet. A drop of rain made its way down his temple and the side of his face, then hung from the end of his chin.

'I need to get to work,' he told Annie and Gemma.

Annie turned to look back down at George. It was odd, having her look down on him.

'Go on then,' she said. 'We'll be fine.' He noticed that she said 'we' – Gemma's sorrow had clearly helped Annie make up her mind.

'Oh,' said George. 'Right.' He pushed his rain-spattered glasses up his nose. 'You two have fun.' And he headed down the hill.

Women, he'd decided long ago, were not really his forte.

Annie and Gemma watched him make his way down the hill away from them. He glanced back a couple of times and they waved. George seemed torn whether to wave back or pretend he hadn't seen. He dipped his head, trudging on down the hill and was lost around the corner.

'So,' said Annie, when he had gone.

'So,' said Gemma, levelly.

The two women – the two ghosts – regarded each other.

'You never told him about the darkness. The men with sticks and ropes.'

Annie shook her head. 'George needs to believe there's something good waiting on the other side.'

'He's got his faith,' nodded Gemma. 'I seen the pendant round his neck.' Then her eyes lit up with a thought. 'But his faith isn't enough. He doesn't like what he is.'

'He can't bear it,' said Annie. 'No, that's the thing.

He *does* bear it. He carries it round with him all the time.'

'It's a curse,' said Gemma.

'It's not *him* that bothers him,' said Annie. 'It's what he can do to other people. Hurt them, kill them… Or give them what he's got.'

'He's a good boy,' said Gemma.

'Yeah,' said Annie. 'He and Mitchell, they're the best.'

She found Gemma smiling at her, eyes twinkling with mischief. 'You're sweet on them.'

'No!' Annie protested, feeling her cheeks flush with embarrassment and anger. 'No!' She pulled her cardigan tightly round herself. 'They're just my friends. I don't think anything else.'

'Course not,' said Gemma, her eyes still twinkling. 'I never thought you did.'

'Well, yeah,' said Annie. 'It's ridiculous. And it's not like either of them sees anything in me. I'm like a sister or something.'

'They're both very protective of you,' said Gemma.

Annie nodded. 'Yeah, that's what it is.' She felt a pang inside her. Was that all they felt for her – that she needed protecting? That she couldn't cope on her own. That's exactly how George had been this morning, when she'd wanted him to speak to Gemma. Well she'd show him; she'd spend all day with Gemma and they'd both be fine.

She looked up, found Gemma still watching her

with fascination. 'Anyway,' said Annie. 'It doesn't matter. So don't say anything to them.'

'What would I tell them?' asked Gemma, all innocence, that glint still in her eyes.

'Yeah,' agreed Annie, feeling uncomfortable. 'Anyway. What do you want to do? We could go for a walk, or go back to the house.'

'Whatever you want to do,' smiled Gemma. 'I don't want to be any bother.'

Annie wanted to go back to the house; she hated being outside. It felt like people were watching, waiting to attack. The more she tried to ignore the sensation, the more it felt like there were people hiding, just out of view. But she couldn't admit that to Gemma. She knew Gemma wouldn't say anything, she'd go along with whatever Annie wanted. But she'd have the same pitying look in her eyes as Mitchell and George. Poor, fearful Annie always hiding herself away. She knew she was being silly, irrational, but the more they pitied her and didn't say anything, the more she wanted to hide.

'Let's go to the park,' she said quickly, before she'd had time to consider the idea.

Gemma nodded. 'Whatever you want,' she said.

'Yeah,' said Annie, decided now. 'Let's go to –'

'– the park.'

They stood on the grass beside a bench, the park laid out before them.

Gemma gasped, reaching out for the back of the

bench to steady herself. Her eyes opened wide as she took in where they were. Then she smiled in awe at Annie.

'Oh yeah,' said Annie. 'We can do stuff like this. Bit more fun than walking.'

Gemma nodded, trying to take it in. 'You just think where you want to be…' she said.

'Kind of,' said Annie. 'You fix a picture of it in your mind. You sort of feel yourself being there. And then you are. You sort of just do it.'

She shrugged, turning to lead Gemma up the slope of slick, wet grass, into the whispering rain. She didn't feel the wet or cold but lowered her head into the rain anyway. Like leaping across town just by wanting to, she thought she'd be able to feel the rain by force of will. But Annie couldn't allow that, couldn't let herself go. She knew she'd unravel into the air, that she had to cling on tight to her existence.

Gemma followed her, not saying a word, lost in her own morbid thoughts. The further you got from the safety of the house, the more you explored the world of the living, the more you felt your detachment from it. That, at least, was how Annie felt these days. There'd been times when the boys had made her forget that she'd died, brought her out of herself. But that feeling never lasted.

She reached the crest of the hill and looked back at the slope they had climbed and the city stretching out behind it. The modern office blocks and apartments, the smart Victorian terraces, the rise of what had once been the castle. Annie had been in love with Bristol, when she'd still been alive.

She turned to Gemma, to find the woman wasn't there.

Annie looked all round, but Gemma had vanished. Annie stood alone on the bare hilltop – utterly alone. 'Gemma?' she called out. '*Gemma*!?'

'What is it?' said Gemma, running over to join her.

Annie gasped for breath, desperately relieved. 'I couldn't see you,' she said. 'I thought you'd left me on my own.'

'Where would I go?' said Gemma.

Annie felt stupid for having got in so much of a panic. 'You might have gone to see someone you used to know,' she said. 'I used to do that.'

Gemma slowly shook her head, that stern look in her eyes that seemed to burn right through Annie. 'No,' she said simply. 'Anyone who mattered is dead.' There was almost a smile on her face, at the irony of it.

'I'm sorry,' said Annie.

Gemma turned away from her. 'Don't be,' she said. They stared out across the city to the suburbs beyond.

'Can you see where you used to live?' Annie asked, eager to change the subject.

Gemma blinked, coming out of whatever spell she'd been under. She looked around, then pointed off in the distance. 'St George's is over there.'

Annie nodded, surprised. That wasn't where Gemma had been staring. She'd been transfixed by another suburb, on the other side of the city. Annie tried to make it out. She turned, and found Gemma staring again at the same old, redbrick cluster of houses.

'Is that Ashton Park?' said Annie, trying to get her bearings. Gemma didn't reply, just carried on staring, eyes wide.

'They're going to regenerate it all over there,' said Annie. 'It's been in the *Daily Press*. Part of their big plan to manage the traffic. Another lane for the M32 where it needs it, a new school with an Olympic-sized pool. And the old student houses will be knocked down to make way for this new road.'

Gemma didn't say anything. Annie knew it wasn't very interesting, but she didn't know what else to say. She'd found it hard enough herself to come back from the dead without having to see her city so changed. Ten years, she thought. Gemma hadn't even seen the Millennium Night fireworks, which seemed such a lifetime ago.

And then Gemma gasped. Annie turned. Gemma had one hand up to her breast, gripping the flesh over her heart. Her eyes were open wide, her lips trembled as she tried to speak or breathe. She quivered like she'd been struck by lightning. Then she collapsed onto the wet grass. Her hat rolled down the hill.

Annie ran over, skidding down beside Gemma, cradling her head. 'What is it?' she begged, terrified. 'Gemma, what's happening?' Gemma shook heavily beneath her. The light was going out in her eyes.

'Stop it!' Annie shouted. 'You've got to stop it!' She grabbed Gemma's shoulders hard. 'You can't have a heart attack when you're already dead!'

Gemma suddenly sat up, arching back and stretching her head up to the sky. She gagged, and the breath finally got through. It wheezed through her mouth and then growled out again. Gemma sat there for a moment, then slumped into Annie's arms.

Annie cradled her, Gemma's lacquered hair like vinyl against her own skin. Gemma breathed ragged breaths, a river of tears down her face.

'It's all right,' Annie cooed. 'It's going to be all right.'

Gemma twitched in her embrace, a spasmodic movement as she shook her head.

'The road,' she said. 'The road.'

Chapter
FIVE

Mitchell didn't like being in Intensive Care. The Intensive Care Unit was on the top floor of the hospital and most people – patients and staff – never went anywhere near it. It lacked the bustle and vibrancy of anywhere else in the building. The lights were kept low, noise to a minimum, almost like a church. Even the hospital's chapel felt less sombre than this place.

'Hello?' called Mitchell as he stepped into the dark catacomb. Lights winked in the gloom, the machines sitting watch over the bodies in the beds. There were two rows of them on either side of the unit, a dozen bodies in total. Pale and perfectly still, they each slept their own artificial sleep. The machines breathed for them and fed them nutrients through tubes. They monitored their hearts and brains.

A coma was a cruel parody of life as a vampire. The bodies around the Intensive Care Unit were on the same cusp of life and death as Mitchell, not quite one or the other. But while Mitchell feasted on blood to keep himself alive, these bodies were far more odious parasites. True, they were just plugged into the wall, the machines running off the mains. But they also needed so much tending.

At intervals throughout the day, nurses would come to check over the bodies, massaging their limbs and moving the sleepers so their muscles didn't wither away. There was something eerie and graceful about that exercise regime. Mitchell had nightmares about it. Paralysed yet alive, unable to scream as weary hands shaved and scrubbed and pressed him. Being a vampire didn't mean living for ever, it meant retaining independence. So this wretched state terrified him – being helpless, weak, reliant on others.

But it was also the toll on other people that Mitchell found so appalling. He had seen the families and loved ones shuffling up the stairs into this dark vault. The parents who'd grown old, developed cancer and died while a beloved daughter slept on. He had seen the muted conversations as families tore themselves apart making awful decisions. There were those who decided to turn off the machines, and those who chose never to visit again. And worst of all were the ones who came back, week after week. Mitchell could see the hope being leeched from them, as if each sleeping body devoured it.

'Hello?' he called again, louder this time. He felt cold, and nervous. That same feeling he'd had in the vault the previous day – that dread sense of being watched. Was this another test?

'Mitchell,' said a voice from the darkness. Mitchell grinned.

'Gail,' he said. 'They said I was needed.'

Gail stepped forward, the lights from the machines spotlighting her in pink and green. She was a pretty black woman with ample curves and a serious look in her eyes. Mitchell had once tried to casually chat her up. She'd cut him dead and they'd never got on since.

'Yeah,' said Gail, regarding him. 'I thought it would be someone else.'

'Sorry,' said Mitchell.

Gail shrugged. 'Can't be helped. It's Mrs Wright.' She nodded at a woman who couldn't have been much older than 60, sitting by the bed of a sleeping old man. 'Husband collapsed this morning,' Gail sighed. 'Been in A&E, then they brought him up here after lunch. Only because we had a free bed. It's all about money, isn't it?'

'What isn't?' said Mitchell.

'Most things,' she said, sniffily. 'If you're not blinded to it.'

Mitchell grinned. 'Blinded to what?'

'Heteronormative patriarchy.' Gail regarded him coolly. 'You don't even know what that is.'

'No,' Mitchell admitted. He didn't want to laugh at Gail, so he turned away. Mitchell stared not at the man sleeping peacefully on the bed but at the woman sat beside him, the one who was suffering.

'Mrs Wright needs to get home,' said Gail. 'Pick up some things. It might be a long night. So take her back down to the reception and find her a taxi.'

'OK,' said Mitchell. 'I can handle that.'

Gail wrinkled her nose at him. 'Pleased with yourself, aren't you?' she said. Then she shrugged. 'Guffy singled you out.'

'Who?'

'Guffy,' said Gail. 'I guess you're on first-name terms.'

Mitchell laughed. 'You mean Dr McGough? God no, nothing like that. We haven't even spoken. He probably doesn't know I exist.'

Gail narrowed her eyes at him. 'Yeah,' she said. 'You can make yourself invisible when you want to.'

Mitchell regarded her coolly. 'And what's that supposed to mean?'

'That you've been watched,' said Gail. 'That you've been noticed. Women go near you and nasty shit happens.'

'Hey,' said Mitchell, raising his hands. 'I'm not that kind of guy.'

'You're all charm first,' Gail told him. 'When you've got what you want, the women are in pieces.'

'Who have you been talking to?' said Mitchell,

scrolling in his mind through all the people he might have offended. He couldn't think of anyone in particular.

Gail prodded him with a finger. 'Just know you're being watched,' she told him. 'If there's a formal complaint, you won't be invisible any more. Not even Guffy will save you.'

She marched off, leaving Mitchell stood there, baffled as much as anything else. Gail must have got the wrong end of the stick somewhere. Or someone had been slagging him off. Or, the thought struck him, someone had finally pieced together the mysteries of the last few months. The deaths of Lauren and Becca, both of whom he'd been seen with.

Mitchell's blood ran cold. Had he finally been noticed? There was no Herrick to protect him now.

He ran his fingers through his long, lank hair and took a deep breath. No, they couldn't have worked it out yet. If they had, Gail wouldn't confront him on her own. She and her mates would come at him together, wielding pitchforks and flaming torches. Until they did that, he'd just have to keep a low profile. And get on with his job.

Mitchell made his way over to Mrs Wright. She ignored him, even when he stood over her. He watched her hold her husband's pale hand, muttering what might have been a prayer or just the news her husband had missed out on while he'd been sleeping.

'Mrs Wright,' said Mitchell. She didn't look up.

Mitchell glanced round at the next bed. A tall woman of about 30 slept soundly, breathing controlled by machine. Mitchell looked at the board above the bed. Rebecca Hywel-Jones had been born in 1981. She had spent more than one-third of her life in a coma.

Mitchell gazed down at the pale, placid face, the skin almost translucent and grey. She might have been a corpse were it not for the automated breathing. There was something about her, too. Something Mitchell could almost taste in the air. A sense of her, the real her, floating just out of reach.

He whirled round, quickly, feeling the eyes on him, expecting Gail to be watching. Instead, in the darkness, he saw someone else.

A skinny black teenager in a loose-fitting T-shirt stared back at him with baleful eyes. Mitchell had never seen this gaunt figure before, sad, deep-set eyes and no meat on him. They stared at each other. Mitchell started to say something...

And the boy wasn't there any more.

Mitchell looked round, but there was no black teenager. The Intensive Care Unit was silent and unmoving. The machines kept their vigil, the sleepers breathed their artificial breaths. Mrs Wright muttered to her husband.

Mitchell sighed. Had he seen a ghost? Of course, he thought, a place like this would be haunted. The boy had looked startled, surprised to be noticed.

You generally only saw ghosts when they wanted to be seen. But Mitchell had been friends with Annie long enough now that he might have grown more attuned to spotting them.

That was certainly easier than the other possibility, that there was some skinny kid up here, lurking in the darkness. Mitchell let his predatory senses reach out, round the ward. His mind bristled at the inanimate bodies but, bar the weak heart battering inside Mrs Wright, he could not sense anyone else around.

A ghost then, he decided. He'd endeavour to keep out of its way.

'Mrs Wright,' he said more firmly. 'They said you wanted to go home for some things.'

The mutter stopped. She still gripped the old man's hand as she looked up at Mitchell. He was struck by the steely glint in her eyes.

'It's all right for him,' she said bitterly. 'He could always sleep through anything.'

Mitchell reached down to take her hand. 'Come on,' he said, helping her stand. 'Why don't you tell me about it?'

'You're a porter,' she said as they stood in the noisy lift. Notices told them about fines in the car park and the importance of washing their hands.

Mitchell looked down at the frail Mrs Wright. Her hands shook as she gripped her walking stick. But she smiled up at him benignly.

'Yeah,' he said. 'Best job in the world.'

Mrs Wright smiled, showing yellow teeth. 'My husband was a porter here,' she said. 'For almost thirty years.'

'Must have been before my time,' said Mitchell.

'Same job,' said Mrs Wright. 'The things no one else will do.'

'True,' said Mitchell. 'When did he retire?'

The smile faded from her face. 'He didn't.'

'I'm sorry,' said Mitchell.

Mrs Wright nodded.

'What happened?' asked Mitchell. 'If you don't mind me asking.'

Mrs Wright sighed. 'I suppose you could say that the job got to him, in the end. All the people you have to help. The horrid things you see. People in pieces.'

'We put them back together,' said Mitchell.

'Not always,' said Mrs Wright. 'It's like standing against the tide.'

Mitchell had felt the same thing himself. He stood outside the normal order of things. A vampire didn't get old or sick, didn't slowly come apart like ordinary mortals. The very word 'mortals' – things that die. Even the healthy ones – the children born here, the kids just in for injections, the young doctors who were still so keen – all of them faced the inevitable. They were all on their way out.

'What happened?' he asked Mrs Wright, feeling a kinship for her husband.

She sighed. 'Nothing in particular,' she said. 'It just got to him. The things he'd seen and done. The misery of sickness. The injustice of it ate away at him. He used to get so angry.'

'It can be cruel,' agreed Mitchell. 'The wrong people get sick.'

'Yes,' she said. 'Then it was just too much. His temper got worse, and his drinking.'

'He saw something,' said Mitchell. 'Something especially bad.'

Mrs Wright looked up at Mitchell, fixing him with her beady, piercing eyes. 'Nothing in particular,' she told him. 'He would have told me if he had. He told me everything.'

Mitchell nodded. 'I'm sorry.'

Mrs Wright patted his hand. 'You remind me of him, a bit,' she said. 'You pretend not to care, but there's all that fire inside you.'

Mitchell grinned. 'You're pretty fiery yourself, Mrs Wright.'

She grinned up at him, cheeks flushed. 'I'm old enough to be your granny.'

'You think?' he said. 'Besides, I like an older woman. More experience.'

Mrs Wright smiled up at him, but he saw the sadness in her eyes. He'd let her escape her sorrows only for a moment. But she couldn't escape the tide.

The lift pinged and the doors slid open revealing the drab ground-floor corridor. In silence, Mitchell led Mrs Wright through to reception and found her a seat. He then used the phone on the wall to call a taxi.

'Five minutes,' he told her, coming back over to her chair. 'He'll come in here to find you.'

'Thank you,' said Mrs Wright, still consumed by sadness. Mitchell loitered, not wishing to leave her.

'I'm all right,' she told him. 'But thank you for taking the time.' She hesitated. 'And also…'

'Yes?' said Mitchell.

'Don't get old,' she told him.

Mitchell smiled down at her. 'I won't,' he promised, and went back to his work.

George came to find him at the end of his shift. They had glimpsed each other at various moments, but both been too busy to stop. The hospital staff were all running themselves ragged, desperate not to be singled out by Dr McGough.

'So,' grinned George. 'Still here?'

'Seem to be,' said Mitchell. They ducked into the men's locker room, where they stashed their civilian clothes. George leaned against one wall, arms folded, as Mitchell prised open his locker.

'There was some·junior doctor yesterday,' said Mitchell. 'Dropped a patient's file, pages going everywhere. All witnessed by Dr McGough. Bloke hasn't been in today.'

George looked appalled. 'He's been fired?'

'Word is he took a day sick,' said Mitchell. 'But I

heard the nurses say he's not coming back.' He ran a hand through his long hair. 'They couldn't have been more delighted. Like it meant it wouldn't be them. Christ, what's happening to us all?'

'They're making a whole load of accusations upstairs,' said George. 'People filing complaints about people they've worked with for years. There's all these stories of unexplained deaths and paperwork going missing. It's like living under the Nazis.'

'No it isn't,' said Mitchell darkly. 'Not yet.'

George stared at him.

Mitchell shrugged. 'Anyway,' he said, 'we know why the paperwork's gone missing.'

'It's not just vampire stuff,' George pouted. 'Really, there's something else going on. There's been three complaints about Sarah on reception – she's not even due in today. And everywhere you go people are watching. Whispering. Looking for stuff to tag on you.'

Mitchell nodded. 'I think I had that upstairs. You know Gail?'

'Lesbian Gail? Kaz's girlfriend?'

Mitchell shook his head. 'She's a lesbian?'

George sighed. 'I know. There are some women out there who don't want to sleep with you.'

'Not possible,' grinned Mitchell.

'That,' said George, 'is why you're getting a reputation.'

'I am not!' said Mitchell. 'Am I?'

George looked at him levelly. 'We're meant to be keeping a low profile, remember. You can't enjoy this!'

'No,' said Mitchell. 'This is all getting out of hand. I keep feeling I'm being watched.'

'Yeah,' said George. 'Everyone's paranoid. '

'No,' said Mitchell. 'I mean it. I'm being watched. I was down in the vault for some blood yesterday…'

'Oh brilliant,' said George. 'And someone saw you.'

'No,' said Mitchell. 'I wasn't there for that. They needed blood on one of the wards. But when I was down there… Well, it was just this feeling. There was no one around, but I knew they were watching.'

'But somehow that's a completely different thing from paranoia,' said George.

'Yeah,' Mitchell insisted. 'A completely different thing.'

'All right,' said George. 'So who?'

'I think I saw a ghost up in ICU,' said Mitchell.

George shrugged. 'What did they say?'

'Nothing,' said Mitchell. 'Vanished soon as I saw him.'

'And that's who was watching you yesterday?'

Mitchell was about to say no. But he'd felt the same creeping coldness both times, the same eerie sense of someone watching him. 'Maybe,' he said.

'What are we going to do?' said George.

'Nothing,' said Mitchell. 'We can't let ourselves be noticed.'

'So what?' said George. 'You're not going downstairs to get blood, unless someone else sends you to get some?'

'George,' said Mitchell, 'I was watched.'

'Fine,' said George crossly. 'How long do you think you can last? It'll eat you up. And then you'll eat someone. People will notice you then.'

Mitchell glowered at him. 'What do you suggest?'

'I don't know,' said George. 'But there *are* things the hospital could do better. If Guffy could just concentrate on those bits and not be looking at everyone...'

'Guffy,' muttered Mitchell.

'That's what everyone calls him,' said George. 'Makes it sound like he farts a lot.'

'Think he's too clenched to let anything out,' smiled Mitchell. 'What can we give him? There's someone you want to point the finger at? '

'No!' said George. 'But if we just give him something to look at. There's a whole load of odd stuff in the autopsy paperwork. There's got to be something there.'

'You mean lead him to the vampires.'

'Yeah, right,' said George. 'Of course not. But there's loads of odd stuff in the files. We just need to find something that will tie him up. Let us get on with our work.'

Mitchell nodded. 'All right,' he said. 'So where do we start?'

George sighed. 'I was hoping you'd tell me.'

Mitchell stared at him for a moment, then slowly shook his head. 'George,' he said. 'I'm going home.'

Mitchell just wanted to chill out that evening, put his feet up in front of the telly. He'd forgotten until he stepped through the front door that they had a guest staying.

'Hi!' he beamed at Gemma, as convincingly as he could. She sat on the sofa in the living room, a thousand pieces of jigsaw scattered on the table in front of her.

'Hi,' she wheezed, struggling to get to her feet. 'You want me to fix you something to eat?'

'Huh?' said Mitchell. 'No, I'm fine, thanks.' The smile dropped. 'Are you feeling all right?'

Gemma took a step backwards. 'I'm fine,' she told him.

But she didn't look it. Her eyes seemed dark and deep-set, like she had been crying. Sweat beaded on her forehead, under the immaculate lacquer of her hair.

'She had a funny turn,' said Annie, emerging from the kitchen, arms full of various board games. The house had a motley collection, some bought new because they'd seemed like a good idea, others from second-hand shops where they'd made Mitchell smile. The Vampire Game from Waddingtons had proven to be one of their favourites.

'I'm fine,' Gemma declared again, sitting back

down. She studiously ignored them both, transfixed by the jigsaw.

'She's better than she was,' Annie told Mitchell, not lowering her voice. 'But we were at the park—'

'You went to the park?' laughed Mitchell. Annie had barely left the house recently.

'We were at the park,' Annie persevered. 'And she had some kind of fright. Something to do with the new road they're building through Ashton Park.'

'It's not through Ashton Park,' said Mitchell. 'It's more just outside.' He glanced back at Gemma, poised over the jigsaw. She continued the pretence that she couldn't hear them talking about her, but the sweat still beaded on her forehead. Mitchell watched her separate the edge pieces from the rest. Her hands trembled as she worked.

'What's so bad about the road?' he asked her. Gemma flinched, almost imperceptibly. But she didn't acknowledge what he'd said.

'She wouldn't tell me either,' said Annie. 'I brought her back here, and she just sat on the sofa. I didn't know what to do with her. I only just thought of the games.'

Annie placed the games down on the floor beside the table. Gemma looked round at her, annoyed by the disturbance.

'Sorry,' said Annie, backing away. 'We only want to help.'

Gemma waved her away with one simple movement of her hand. 'I know, dear,' she said, absorbed by the jigsaw again. 'I don't want to be any trouble.'

Annie returned to Mitchell, hovering by the front door. 'See?' she said.

Mitchell considered, watching Gemma as she assembled the top edge of the jigsaw. Blobs of random colour joined up to make the sky.

'It's been exhausting,' said Annie. Mitchell looked at Annie, and yes, she did look paler.

'Don't sweat it,' he said. 'We can't force her. She'll tell us when she wants to.'

Mitchell spent the next couple of hours in his room trying to read a book. Annie sat at the end of the bed, and when he looked up she only mugged at him. He read the same sentence again and again.

'OK,' he said at last, dropping the book on his lap.

'OK,' agreed Annie.

'We should go downstairs,' said Mitchell.

'Yeah,' said Annie. Neither of them made any move.

'I've been at work all day,' said Mitchell. 'And Gemma just wants to do her jigsaw. Being with her, it's like she drains the life out of you.'

'I feel drained,' nodded Annie. 'And I'm not even alive.'

'I don't mean drained,' said Mitchell. 'She's nice. And her being upset, it makes me feel guilty about just wanting to put my feet up.'

'I feel guilty too,' said Annie. 'Nothing I do makes her feel any better. I'm drawn into her black cloud. And I've got nothing to be upset about.'

Mitchell sat up. 'We have to help her,' he said.

'Yes,' agreed Annie. 'How do we help her?'

'There's something about this road,' he said.

'Or where it's being built,' said Annie.

'Yeah,' said Mitchell. 'But she lived in St George's. The road doesn't go anywhere near.'

'I asked her if she ever lived in Ashton Park,' said Annie. 'But she said she never did.'

'What else did she say?' asked Mitchell.

Annie considered. 'Nothing,' she said.

'Nothing at all?'

'I asked her everything I could think of,' said Annie. 'And she just sort of sat there. We both sat there, not saying anything. It's so much effort not to do anything! And then I thought of the jigsaw.'

'She seems to like doing that.'

'Yeah,' muttered Annie. 'I thought it was something we could both do. But she sort of took over.'

'What we need,' said Mitchell, stroking the stubble on his chin, 'is someone to bring her out of herself. Someone she can tell anything.'

They both considered this. Then Annie clapped her hands together, a brilliant grin on her face. 'George!' she said.

Mitchell nodded. 'George.'

*

They went downstairs together and didn't even glance at Gemma. She sat in the living room, the jigsaw far from complete, the picture coming together. An old-fashioned steam-powered tractor in a field on a warm summer's day.

Annie and Mitchell walked through to the kitchen and began to go through the cupboards. Mitchell loaded a tin of beans and a box of fajitas onto the counter, Annie fetched chicken and fresh chillies from the fridge. Without a word they worked around one another, Annie almost shaking as she held in the laughter.

'What are you two up to?' said Gemma from the kitchen doorway. Mitchell and Annie exchanged grins. Annie looked ready to burst, so Mitchell turned to face Gemma, biting down his smile.

'Hi,' he said. 'George will be home in half an hour. We thought we'd have Mexican waiting.'

'Can I help?' said Gemma, gliding between him and Annie to take the chopping board from the wall.

'Really, you don't need to do anything,' Mitchell told her. Annie's eyes gleamed with tears.

'I want to,' Gemma told him. 'You don't mind?'

'No,' said Mitchell. 'And that's very good of you,' he said to her back as she set to the chillis. Annie joined him at the door of the kitchen. 'I know George will really appreciate it.'

At that very moment they heard the key in the front door. George stepped into the house, weighed down by his bag and his worries. He looked up, startled to find Mitchell and Annie staring at him.

'What?' he said, in a high, scared voice.

'Hi!' said Annie, so excited she even waved at him.

'You're early,' said Mitchell.

George looked at his watch then blinked back at Mitchell. 'Finished at eight,' he said. 'So I'm always back around now.' Then his expression hardened. He put down his bag, shut the front door behind him, and poked his nose into the kitchen.

'What's going on?' he said.

'It was going to be a surprise,' Mitchell said as George barrelled past him.

'Gemma,' said George slowly. 'You're cooking.'

She didn't even turn round. 'Mexican,' she said.

'Mexican?' said George horrified. It was one of his signature dishes.

Gemma stopped chopping the chilli and turned slowly to face him. 'You don't mind?' she said.

'Mind?' he said. 'No, no, it's just fine.' His tone said it was anything but.

Gemma studied him. 'You cook when you get home,' she said. 'It's how you unwind.'

George's whole body sagged. 'Yes,' he said. 'It's just been one of those days. Dr McGough visited Windsor Unit, made a speech to everyone there. Just slipped in casually that he wouldn't close them down if he could avoid it. So now they all think they're out of jobs.'

Gemma sighed. 'I only wanted to help,' she said, turning her head sadly.

'I know,' said George, a whirl of frustration and ingrained good manners. 'It doesn't matter.'

'Course it does!' Gemma declared, grabbing his hand in both of hers. 'You come help make this into a feast!'

George glanced back at Mitchell and Annie, a despairing look on his face. He just wanted the kitchen to himself, so he could work out his frustrations in peace. But he would never have said as much, not until he knew Gemma much better. And Mitchell wasn't going to save him.

'I'll go and get some wine,' said Mitchell.

'What?' said George. 'You can't—'

'It's no trouble,' Mitchell assured him.

'I'll come too,' agreed Annie, linking her arm around Mitchell's.

Mitchell grinned. 'Seems like a fair division of labour.'

'Go on if you're going,' Gemma told them. 'We'll be fine.' She grinned up at George. 'Won't we?'

'Of course,' he said.

Leaving George to his fate, Annie and Mitchell headed for the door. As Mitchell shrugged on his leather jacket, Annie opened the front door then hesitated on the doorstep. Mitchell took her hand and led her out into the night.

As they stopped to close the door behind them, they heard George's muted voice.

'So,' he said to Gemma. 'How was your day, then?'

Annie and Mitchell listened with bated breath. A saucepan clattered as it was put on the stove.

'Well,' they heard Gemma start to say.

Mitchell slammed the door.

Chapter
Six

Annie clung to Mitchell's arm as they made their way up the street and round to the little shop, yet she also beamed, full of excitement that their trick was working. They took their time prowling the aisles, picking up nuts and a jar of olives *con pimiento*. Mitchell perused the meagre selection of wines, Annie ribbing him about how he was such a connoisseur.

All the time, the man behind the counter stroked his fine moustache and watched them. The more Annie teased Mitchell and the more they giggled like kids, the less the man with the moustache seemed pleased.

'Hey,' Mitchell said to him when he finally handed over his basket.

The moustachioed man bleeped the nuts and

olives through the till. As he took the first bottle of Shiraz, he looked up at Mitchell. 'I can get in trouble,' he said, 'for selling alcohol when you're drunk.'

'Should think so too,' agreed Mitchell as he handed over twenty quid. The moustachioed man muttered something as he put together the right change. Mitchell realised what the man had meant.

'I'm not drunk!' he laughed. 'What makes you think that?'

The moustachioed man didn't say anything as he loaded the things Mitchell had bought into a stripy plastic bag.

'I'm not!' Mitchell protested. 'I haven't had anything yet!'

'What was he all about?' he asked Annie as they stepped back out into the street. 'Do I look like I've been drinking?'

'We took a while choosing what we wanted,' said Annie.

'We were just having a laugh,' said Mitchell.

'Yeah,' said Annie. 'But he couldn't see me with you.'

Mitchell stopped in the street to stare at her. He glanced back at the shop, his mouth hanging open, not sure where to start. Annie took him by the hand.

'Come on,' she said. 'Let's see if George has worked his magic.'

They could feel it as they stepped into the house.

The glorious aroma of spice enveloped them as they came in, but so too did the silence. Mitchell and Annie exchanged worried glances and hurried through to the kitchen.

Gemma didn't look up as they entered. She sat at the table, cutlery for four gripped in her right hand.

George was busy ladling dark chicken and chilli into the fajitas, then rolling them up like cigars. He glanced back, flicked a smile on and off, then returned to his work.

Annie and Mitchell took their seats at the table without a word. Mitchell reached for the bottle opener, then found that he'd bought screw-tops. He sloshed wine into the two waiting glasses.

George handing round the plates brought Gemma to her senses. She passed round the cutlery without making eye contact. George took his seat and they sat there, looking down at the pungent, steaming food as if waiting for someone to say grace.

'Well,' said Mitchell at length. 'This looks great.'

'Mmm,' Annie agreed.

George nodded, acknowledging their kindness. Then he looked levelly at Gemma.

'Do you want me to tell them?' he asked her.

Gemma shook her head. A single tear tumbled from her eyelash and skittered down her cheek.

'My son,' she said. They sat there, watching her, steam curling from their plates.

'He was 18,' said George. 'Lived in Ashton Park.'

'Couldn't live with his mum,' said Gemma. 'Had to have his independence. Even when we found out my cancer wasn't getting any better.'

'I'm sorry,' said Mitchell.

Gemma looked up at him suddenly, such bitterness in her eyes. A broad, powerful woman and Mitchell found himself the focus of her anger.

'He died,' said George.

Gemma lowered her eyes. 'They made me do chemotherapy. My hair came out in handfuls. I couldn't even walk.' She let out a sob. 'So I wasn't there. When he needed me.'

'He was living in a squat,' said George. 'The people he was living with, they weren't a good lot. Into drugs and who knows what else. They bullied Lee. One night they tied him up naked, took a whole load of Polaroids and posted them to Gemma.'

'I tried to talk to him,' said Gemma. 'But he would never discuss it. I saw it eating him up. I wanted to help him. And then... And then...'

Gemma's body was wracked by sobbing, but she didn't make a sound. Annie put out a hand to her, but Gemma twitched out of reach as if the touch might burn her. Annie's own eyes were watering, though that might have been the industrial, sulphurous tang coming off Gemma, as if to keep them back. Gemma stared round at them, her eyes awful to behold.

'I see it all the time,' she said. 'I see the rope he used.'

*

George didn't know what to do. He sat there, staring at his food as it got cold. He hated feeling so awkward, especially in his own house. With everything at work and in his life at the moment, this was the last thing that he needed. And yet he would never have dared to protest.

'You can't blame yourself,' said Mitchell.

Gemma snorted. 'Can't I?'

'Of course not,' said Mitchell.

'A thing like that,' agreed George, eager to get this thing sorted. 'It can be hardest on those it leaves behind.'

'You think my cancer killed Lee?' Gemma asked, as if the idea amused her.

'What about his dad?' asked Annie. 'He did have a dad?'

'Not one he ever knew,' said Gemma. She had transformed in the quarter of an hour Annie and Mitchell had spent buying the wine. The broad, statuesque woman had collapsed in on herself. Her perfect poise now seemed warped and twisted by the raging storm within.

'I brought him up,' she said. 'Did what little I could. Dropped out of college, got a job in a pharmacy, just to make sure he got fed. Gave up everything for that boy, not that he'd ever have known it. I made sure I never said anything.'

But George could see it all too perfectly. The son growing up knowing how much of a burden he'd been. You'd never do anything good enough for your mum after what she'd done for you. You'd never outrun the guilt. He could feel it himself, sat at the table with Gemma, having to indulge her misery when he had so many problems of his own.

'You can't blame yourself,' he told her.

'Maybe I was too hard on him,' she said. 'Or I was too soft. There's things I could have done different.' She took a breath and sat up in her seat. George noted the different look in her eyes, the hardness he had glimpsed the previous day.

'But no,' she said firmly. 'I can't blame myself. Not for everything.' She slammed her palm down on the table. 'Come on,' she told them, forcing a smile. 'That food is getting cold.'

No one really spoke for the rest of the evening. Annie tried to do the washing up. She had no sooner started to run the water than Gemma had bumped her out of the way. There was the table to wipe and Annie could have done the drying, but Gemma pretty much shooed her out of the kitchen. Annie joined the boys in the living room, all three of them sat there, not watching the telly.

The jigsaw took up the coffee table, complete but for three missing pieces. They gaped accusingly round the twee image of the tractor, though the pieces been missing when Mitchell had bought the jigsaw.

Gemma finished the washing up and joined them in the living room.

'Do you want to sit down?' Annie asked her, squashing up beside George to make room.

Gemma remained in the doorway, arms folded, regarding the television with distaste. 'I'm fine,' she said without even looking at Annie.

It got worse when the boys had gone up to bed. Annie didn't feel like she could go and look in on them without incurring Gemma's displeasure, but she couldn't bear the thought of another night in the living room with the lights off, waiting endlessly on the dawn. She feared another long conversation, Gemma asking all the right questions to make Annie expose her soul.

Yet still she sat there, in the gloom, watching Gemma crumble the jigsaw back into its box. She so wanted to help, or to shake Gemma out of this awful despair. Annie struggled at the best of times to keep herself from being overwhelmed by all she had lost when she died, and feared Gemma would drag her back down.

'You must have come back because of your son,' said Annie, eager to find a solution. 'The new road must affect his old house.'

Gemma didn't even acknowledge that she'd spoken. As Annie watched, she jiggled the box, shuffling the pieces. Then, with a sigh, she tipped them back on to the table and began the jigsaw once more.

Annie got up and crept into the kitchen. She tugged the top off the kettle but had not even turned on the tap when she found Gemma beside her.

'You're making tea,' said Gemma.

'I know,' said Annie.

'There's no one to drink it,' said Gemma.

'I know,' said Annie, but didn't resist when Gemma took the kettle out of her hands. 'Sorry.'

'There's nothing to be sorry about,' said Gemma. She placed the kettle back on the counter, then returned to the kitchen.

Annie watched her from the doorway of the kitchen, more exasperated than cross. She just wanted to be doing something, to kill the hours until it got light.

A sudden thought struck her. She grinned and –

– found herself somewhere else. The street lamps outside cut blades of light through the blinds in the windows. They picked out the long tables stretching round the room. Computer screens stared dark and blankly as Annie worked her way down each row. Every one of them had been switched off. She knew better than to turn one on; it would be logged, someone would check the records and know that she had been here.

Annie moved on, exploring the maze of high shelves. She passed invisibly through the beams of green light without tripping the library's alarms. The treasure trove of books was organised in the usual unfathomable system. The 300s were social sciences, the 900s were history and geography.

Neither had what she wanted.

'Local history' had books on town planning and old photos, but none of the detail she wanted. A rack held copies of local newspapers in alphabetical order, but nothing that went further back than a week. She was beginning to despair when she found the microfiche machine.

The screen was tall and flat like one of those modern tellies. Black metal panels shrouded the screen, keeping at bay other light sources that might make it harder to read. A complicated mechanism sat under the screen, a bit like the tray of a microscope, bolted to a lens.

It took long enough to find the switch to turn it on. Then Annie had to work out how to fix the slip of acetate into the right bit of the tray. She'd just got the bleached white-on-black writing to appear in focus on the screen when she noticed the tatty folder beside the machine which explained how to work it.

The filing cabinets contained microfiche files for all the local papers going back to before the First World War. Annie fingered through the cardboard files until she found the ones from 1999. A scribbled note on the cover of the folder explained that not all the editions had been copied onto acetate, and that if a researcher had any queries they should contact a member of staff.

That would be difficult in Annie's case. She just prayed that she'd be lucky.

The acetate pages for the first half of 1999 amounted to one small heap. They didn't look much until Annie loaded the first slip of acetate and found how many newspaper pages were crammed onto it. With a sigh she began to wheel through coverage of the heart babies scandal and the Millennium bug.

She handed the pages to Mitchell the moment he opened his eyes. He stared at the notes, written in Annie's girlish handwriting. A whole newspaper report, copied out in full.

'The squat was a house in Bryn Road,' Annie told him. 'Number 8.'

'Great,' said Mitchell. He looked at the clock by the bed. The scarlet digits spelled out 06.57 – a good two hours before the alarm would go off. He glowered at Annie. She grinned back at him.

'The road is being built through it,' she said.

'It'll regenerate the area,' said Mitchell, flopping back onto the bed. From the bedside table he plucked a cigarette.

'They'll demolish that whole row of houses,' said Annie.

'Yeah,' said Mitchell. 'Well, they're probably run down. All those students for so many years.'

'But imagine if it was this place,' Annie insisted.

'They would never dare,' Mitchell told her, flicking cigarette ash across his duvet. 'Totterdown has special historic interest. George already looked that up.'

'Yeah, but imagine if something did happen to the house. What would I be like?'

Mitchell yawned. 'No more nutty than usual.'

She stuck her tongue out at him.

There was a sudden commotion from outside the bedroom door. Something crashed and swore and crashed again out on the landing. Mitchell heard the creak of the bathroom door as it closed and the click of the lock being bolted.

'You already woke George up?' said Mitchell.

'He's got work,' said Annie. 'You're not in till this afternoon.'

'Right,' said Mitchell wearily. 'You could have left me sleeping.'

Annie laughed – like that had been a joke. Mitchell took a long drag on his cigarette. 'Go on, then,' he said. 'Impress me.'

'I'd go crazy,' said Annie. 'I need the house. I can't exist without it. So I'd do anything to save it.'

Mitchell glanced again over Annie's notes. 'Good job you didn't live there, then,' he said.

And then he realised. He sat up, taking a long draw on the cigarette to help his brain catch up. 'Oh,' he said, his amazement becoming a grin. 'Oh, that's brilliant.'

'Yeah,' said Annie, sitting back. 'I am.'

They found Gemma sat downstairs, the jigsaw completed in front of her but for the three missing pieces. She didn't turn her head or show any sign of life as Annie and Mitchell hurried into the living room to join her. Annie plumped down beside her on the sofa and Gemma let out an exhausted sigh.

'Hey,' said Annie.

Gemma nodded her head almost imperceptibly in acknowledgement.

'We've done a bit of digging,' said Annie, grinning with excitement. She nodded her head at Mitchell, keen he be part of this too.

'Yeah,' said Mitchell. 'Annie went to the library. And we think we know why you're here.'

Gemma looked up at him, her eyes dark and awful. Mitchell felt the smile on his face faltering.

'They're going to demolish the street where your son died,' he said. 'It's part of this new road they're building.' Gemma continued to stare up at him, and he couldn't tell if she even heard him. He glanced at Annie.

'I died in this house,' said Annie. 'And I came back as a ghost here.' Gemma turned her head slowly, and Annie couldn't meet her terrible, dark eyes. Instead she looked up at Mitchell again. 'Lee died in that house, didn't he?' she asked him. She looked back at Gemma. 'So…'

'So you think my son is a ghost there,' said Gemma without any hint of emotion. 'And they're going to demolish the house.'

'No,' said Mitchell. 'We won't let them. That's why you're here. It must be. We're going to help you stop the road.'

Gemma stared at him for a long moment. She didn't seem surprised or pleased or horrified. There was no emotion there at all.

'How?' she asked at length. 'How do you stop a road?'

Mitchell grinned. 'Annie's got an idea.'

He turned to Annie, but she gaped back at him. Mitchell nodded, encouraging her to spill out her plan. Annie's mouth opened and closed as she tried to find the words.

'Oh,' said Mitchell to himself. 'OK, we've not got that far yet.' He grinned again, now with embarrassment. 'But knowing the problem, that's the main thing. We can work on the answer together.'

Gemma offered him a crude parody of a smile. 'You don't have any idea.'

'Sure I do,' said Mitchell. He glanced again at Annie, but she had nothing to offer him.

At that moment, George came tumbling down the stairs, hair still wet from the shower, his sweater inside out where he'd pulled it on in too much of a hurry.

'Hi,' he told them as he hesitated by the front door. 'Sorry,' he added. 'Gonna be late again.'

'George,' said Mitchell. 'The very man.'

'What?' squeaked George, just wanting to escape. 'I've got to go.'

'Just answer us this,' said Mitchell. 'We've got to stop the road being built through Ashton Park. How do we do that?'

George stared at him, at Gemma and at Annie. His eyes blinked as he tried to make sense of the question. 'Stop the road being built,' he said to himself slowly. Then he shook his head. 'I wouldn't know where to start.'

Gemma turned to Mitchell. 'You see?' she taunted.

Mitchell still watched George, hovering at the front door, a sly smile on his face. 'But,' he said, and Gemma turned back to face him. 'I think,' said George, drawing it out for this rapt audience, 'I think I know who would.'

'Who?' said Mitchell.

George shrugged. 'Gotta go,' he said, and headed out through the door.

Chapter
SEVEN

George felt pretty pleased with himself on the way to work. It wasn't often he got one over both Mitchell and Annie. They'd spend all day waiting for him to return, by which time he'd have their answer.

He reached the hospital and soon settled down to the morning's chores. A teenage boy needed picking up from X-Ray and wheeling to Fracture Clinic, and there were boxes of surgical gloves to be lugged down to Outpatients.

Dr McGough had not yet been glimpsed in the building, but there was still a palpable tension in the air. Staff watched each other, looking for faults or weaknesses in others that they could use to save themselves.

George found them watching him as he moseyed onto a ward, willing him to slip up somehow. He shrank from the attention, just tried to get on with his job.

'It's all in your head,' he told himself, though he didn't feel very convinced.

The staff seemed to be doing tasks that they would normally give to the porters, just to keep themselves busy. One of the doctors walked alongside a patient in plaster and crutches, the doctor carrying the man's coat and bags. George offered to help – it was unthinkable, a doctor as a beast of burden. But the doctor waved him off, delighted his effort had been noticed.

George found himself with a lull about eleven, where no one had anything for him at all. The other staff continued to watch him, knowing they'd caught him out, that he – not they – had been proven surplus to requirements. It had always been a salacious, gossipy place, but now the constant watching seemed judgemental, too. George was glad to have his assignment from Mitchell so he could still look busy.

'Morning,' he said to Sarah down on reception. 'Not seen Ian, have you?'

'Ian,' Sarah repeated. 'Which Ian were you after?'

'Ian in security,' George told her. 'I, uh, don't know his surname. But you know who I mean. He's…' George dithered about how best to describe him without being rude. 'He, er, looks like he works out. And he's… Well, he's… You know.'

'Got tattoos and a Mohican,' laughed Sarah.

'And earrings,' George added. 'Yeah.'

'They're not earrings, they're *piercings*,' Sarah corrected. She leant forward to whisper to George, 'Is it true he's got them all over?'

'Yeah!' beamed George. 'No,' he added quickly. 'I mean, yeah – that's him. I wouldn't know about anything else.'

'Of course not,' said Sarah, nodding seriously. 'You only want to find him so you can talk about work.'

George glanced round to check who was listening. He shouldn't be doing this in work time – not with everything the way it was. But if he waited until lunch or the end of shift, he might miss Ian for the day. And he couldn't face going back home to Annie and Mitchell tonight without having sorted this out.

'Not exactly,' he said. 'It's more a private matter. You know.'

'You don't need to explain,' Sarah teased.

'Sorry,' said George. 'It's not a big thing, really.'

'Just casual,' said Sarah. 'I know how it is with you boys.'

'Yeah,' said George. 'Everyone's so ready to judge right now. Looking for things they can report up to Guffy.'

'It's discrimination,' said Sarah.

'It shouldn't matter what I want to see him about,' George sighed. 'But for too many people it does.' He was anxious to get on. He nodded at the pages on Sarah's desk, the roster of duties all round the hospital. 'Do you mind…?'

Sarah laughed. 'I don't mind!' she told him. She looked quickly over her shoulder, then leant forward again to whisper. 'Just the opposite. I've even got DVDs.'

George stared at her, baffled. DVDs of what? The smile on Sarah's face faltered.

'Right,' said George, slowly. 'But do you mind telling me if Ian's in today?'

Sarah turned crimson. Then she looked quickly away, busying herself in the paperwork.

'Of course,' she said quickly, flicking the pages. 'You just want to know where he is.'

She flicked the page back again, and George thought she seemed cross. He couldn't think what he'd done, but then a lot of his life was like that.

'I'm sorry,' he said, without knowing what for. 'I didn't mean…'

'No,' Sarah muttered. 'No, of course.' She stabbed at the roster with one finger, without looking back up at George. 'Ian's in all day,' she said. 'If that's all, I've got to get on with my work.'

George made his way down the stairs, puzzling over the conversation. It just didn't make any sense.

He knew, too, that he could relay what had passed between him and Sarah to Mitchell and then it would be obvious. Mitchell would laugh and explain what double meaning George had missed, and then tease him about it for days. George must have intimated by mistake that he wanted sex with Sarah – or worse, that he didn't. It was usually something like that. He just couldn't fathom what or how.

'Georgie!' declared a voice coming up the stairs towards him. George sighed.

'Mossy,' he said, feeling stupid as he said it. Trevor Moss insisted on being called 'Mossy' in the belief that it meant everyone was his mate. A tubby, 30-something orderly, he had nicknames for everyone else in the hospital. It meant everything he said might as well have been given in code.

'Georgie Porgie!' he bellowed again, clapping George on the shoulder. 'Hey?' he said, as if he'd also just made a joke. 'Hey?' he said again.

'Hey,' said George, praying that that would suffice.

'Hey,' said Mossy. 'Your "better half" is avoiding me.'

The 'better half' – he pronounced the quote marks – was Mossy's nickname for Mitchell, on the basis that he and George shared a house. George himself was 'the wife'. Mossy's nicknames for everyone else were just as hilarious.

'Why?' asked George. 'What have you done?'

Mossy laughed and again clapped George on the shoulder. 'Nice one,' he said. 'You're a fighter, George. First rate. Prize specimen. But seriously, I am a mite concerned. Your "better half" signed up for Bowling Club and even paid his dues. But then he's not made it along to any of our fixtures.'

George could not imagine Mitchell going bowling. But he could see him promising anything – even coughing up a few quid – just to get rid of Mossy.

'No idea,' said George. 'You'd have to ask him.'

Mossy laughed again. 'I will, I will. But now I think he's avoiding me. Think old Mossy's good looks must be fading.'

George stared at him. Had Mossy just referred to himself in the third person? 'Sorry,' he said, and made to move on down the stairs. Before he could escape, however, Mossy placed a hand on his shoulder.

'There's another small matter,' the man said. 'You must know what's happening in the old isolation ward.'

'What?' said George, squirming out of Mossy's grip. 'No. Why should I?'

Once – long before George had started locking himself away down there each month – the disused ward had been used for treating patients with infectious diseases like cholera and Spanish flu. Now, nobody went down there and nothing ever happened. That was what made it so perfect for George.

Mossy's brow furrowed. His temples gleamed with a sheen of sweat. 'Oh,' he said. 'Your "better half" intimated to me that you both had some special reason for going down that way.' His eyes twinkled darkly. 'Some kind of unsavoury acts.'

George held his gaze, wondering what Mitchell might have said. If Mossy really knew the truth, he wouldn't confront George about it. He'd more likely call the police, who were all Mitchell's vampire mates anyway. Mossy and his line of enquiry would not be heard of any further.

'*Unsavoury acts*,' said George, stalling for time. 'That's what Mitchell said?'

Mossy's mouth twitched in what might have been a smile. 'Not exactly,' he said. 'I'm not one to judge. You boys have got your thing. Just wish I had your success rate with the ladies!'

George nodded. So Mitchell had made out they used the isolation ward for sex. He wondered who Mossy thought they had sex with, or if he thought it was different women each time. It struck him that the man was bristling with envy, that he might dare to investigate, even get in on the act himself.

'It's not what you think,' he assured Mossy. 'Mitchell probably made it sound more than it is.'

Mossy looked horrified. 'I wasn't wanting to join in! Heaven forbid! I've my own preferred avenues of interest.'

'Of course,' said George, glad the man was too proud to admit his envy. 'I just mean we don't go down there a lot.'

'Good,' said Mossy. 'I mean, well, that's all right then. It won't make any difference then.'

George felt his heart sinking. 'What won't?'

'Them locking it all up,' Mossy told him. 'Can't go

down there without the express affirmative from the new big cheese. Guff-Bag will allow no exceptions. That's what it says on the memo.' Mossy grinned. 'He likes his memos, doesn't he? All this stuff about files going missing. And stationery pinched from ICU. Disciplinary offence now, apparently. Borrowing a stapler.'

George tried not to let on the panic growing inside him. Mossy grinned at him, delighted at his own comic shtick. 'What does Guffy want with the old isolation ward?' George asked him.

Mossy shrugged up at him. 'Isn't that what I'm asking you? If you find out, I wouldn't mind knowing.' He tapped the side of his nose. 'Always like to know what's going on, Georgie boy. Remember, you're being watched.'

He slapped George once more on the back and then made his way up the stairs.

Ian wasn't in the security office, down in the bowels of the basement. George got one of the other security guys to check the roster, double-checking that Sarah had not misdirected him. But no, the roster clearly said that Ian was due on duty. He'd been seen earlier, too.

'Probably in the canteen,' said the other security guy, glancing over the bank of CCTV screens on the off-chance that they would spot him. George looked at the screens himself, not sure what good the fuzzy images might do. One of the screens showed the passageway outside the isolation ward. There'd been no camera there the last time he'd locked himself in. Or had there?

A chill ran through him. The security guy might have noticed him flinch. George stepped forward, trying to make it all look like one natural movement. 'Canteen,' he said. 'Right.'

'Or,' said the security guy, 'he could be out having a smoke.'

George pointed to the appropriate screen. 'There's no one out the front, is there?'

The security guy shrugged. 'Doesn't smoke cigarettes, you know what I mean? So he doesn't smoke them there.'

George considered. 'Do you mean marijuana?'

The security guy swivelled round on his swivel chair. He stared up at George with dark and beady eyes. 'You wanting to buy some, are you?'

George gulped. 'No,' he said. 'I don't do that sort of thing.' Which was true, but also what he needed to tell a guy who worked in security. Did this guy – Joe, his badge said – think he could catch George out so easily?

'Hmm,' Joe considered, the disappointment evident on his face. 'Everyone's behaving these days.'

George nodded. 'So where will I find him? Ian, I mean.'

'Dunno,' said the security guy. 'Won't show up on any of the screens if he knows what's good for him.

So he could be anywhere.' He sighed. 'Dr McGough wants us putting in more cameras all around the place. Doesn't like there being gaps. But we know exactly what's happening at any time.'

'You don't know where Ian is,' said George.

'True,' said the security guy. 'But then Ian's a professional. He knows how to play these things.'

'Thank you,' said George. 'You've been a great help.'

'No bother,' said the security guy. 'Come back if you change your mind.'

George was already heading back the way he'd come, so didn't ask what he'd have to change his mind about.

Ian wasn't in the canteen. The bored guy on the till hadn't seen him and didn't know who he was anyway. As George described the Mohican and tattoos and piercings, the few diners turned round to stare. George, aware he needed to get back to work, and aware of what felt like a net closing around him as the hospital looked for victims, stared back at them irritably.

'Ian,' said a posh voice.

George turned to find Dr McGough stood behind him, and almost let out a shriek.

'Hi,' he managed to say.

Dr McGough looked up at George, fixing him with beady little eyes. George held his gaze, trying for the life of him not to glance at the gleaming bald head and the ridiculous flap of hair pinned across it. The carnation in the lapel of the administrator's tweed lapel smelled fresh – George thought it must have been picked that morning. He could also tell McGough used two different aftershaves and a peppermint toothpaste.

'You're looking for Ian,' said McGough.

'Yeah,' said George, mouth hanging open. 'He's got a Mohican and piercings. Not that there's anything wrong with that. Is there?'

McGough continued to scrutinise George, as if weighing up whether to sack him immediately or to torture him first. George found his eyes watering with the effort to gaze back. He blinked, glancing upwards, right at the comb-over which so failed to hide the administrator's forehead.

George wanted to laugh, to cry out, to do anything, but he bit down on his lip and kept looking up, as if he'd almost meant to gaze up at the ceiling.

'Are you Danny?' asked McGough.

'No,' said George, looking back down. 'Who's Danny?'

McGough's eyes glittered. 'Oh,' he said mysteriously, 'I must be getting mixed up. Ian said tall and glasses.'

George's heart sank. Had he been singled out already? 'Ian talked to you about me?' he asked.

McGough smiled a benign smile. 'He's very fond of you,' he said. 'That's why this is so tough. He wants you to be part of it with him.'

George stared at him – at the eyes, not the comb-over – and tried to make sense of what he'd got himself caught up in. Had Ian been caught smoking drugs and given George's name to Dr McGough?

'I didn't do anything he said I did,' George told the administrator.

McGough smiled. 'You're finding this difficult, too,' he said kindly. 'That's not surprising. Have you talked to him?'

'Um,' said George. 'I want to. Do you know where he is?'

McGough nodded. 'He's in the old smoking room on the second floor. I think he'd be glad of you there.'

George thanked him and hurried off. He couldn't get away fast enough.

By the time he reached the old smoking room, George felt like he wanted to faint. His hand jittered as he reached for the handle of the door. He had made such a meal of his short conversation with Dr McGough, and now his cards must be marked. The best he could hope for was that he'd lose his job, that he'd have to start all over again. But what if they delved further than just his professional worth, and discovered his secret?

He shook his head, trying to clear the panic. He could do nothing about it now. With a deep breath, he opened the door of the old smoking room and marched smartly inside.

A roomful of women stared back at him. They were all sat round a large table, in the midst of some important meeting. There were people from all levels of the hospital – a couple of consultants, a few doctors and nurses, some of the admin staff. They had coffee and biscuits and stacks of documents, and the meeting had clearly been going on some time.

'Um,' said George, staring at them in horror. There were also three men in attendance. George spotted Ian across the table and instinctively raised his hand to wave.

Ian, perplexed, waved back. Everyone was watching.

Beside Ian was Kaz, the lesbian nurse with the blonde braids and earrings. She grinned at George and got out of her chair. 'You two can sit together,' she said. 'I'll sit somewhere else.'

She pressed round the backs of the other people and found an empty chair. All eyes returned to George, still hovering in the doorway.

'Come on,' said Kaz. 'Take a seat. We're all friends in here.'

George nodded, too embarrassed to do anything else. He squeezed round behind the other attendees and took the chair beside Ian. Ian stared at him, a baffled grin on his face, but didn't say anything in front of the others.

'Sorry,' George whispered. 'Wanted a word. Didn't mean to interrupt.'

He turned back round to face the meeting. And saw the whiteboard up by the door. It showed a roughly drawn diagram of reproductive organs, a man's beside a woman's. Above them was written in friendly, block letters, 'Gay Parenting Group'.

George gaped. He glanced quickly round the table again, taking in which of his colleagues were gay. Some he already knew, but a few were surprising. One of the consultants winked at him. George mouthed *hello* back, not knowing quite what else to do.

'So,' said the other consultant, continuing where she'd left off. 'The difference between IVF and ICSI is the quality of the sperm.' The women round the table nodded, taking this in. A few scribbled notes on the documents in front of them.

George sat quietly while the meeting continued. They discussed the problems one of the women doctors had had. She didn't say anything herself, just nodded, a terrible look in her eyes.

'No one makes it on the first go,' said the woman next to the silent doctor. There were murmurs of assent.

George sat, enthralled and horrified in equal measure as it all spilled out, all the ways that conception could go wrong, the turmoil of going through the IVF process and how it ate people up. He found himself feeling wretched for not knowing about any of this when it seemed so common. And for having been so selfish about his job and his own condition. These women and the three men had their own share of grief. They all got on with their lives in the meantime and their colleagues were none the wiser.

Everyone, George realised, had their problems to deal with.

'Yeah,' said Ian after the meeting, as they all milled about around the coffee and last remaining biscuits. 'I know a lot about direct action. Police broke my arm in three places.'

He didn't seem bitter, thought George, but proud.

'And how long does it take to set up some kind of protest?' George asked, dunking a Bourbon into his coffee.

'About three months,' said Ian.

George looked up at him in surprise, then back down in time to see the end break off his biscuit and float just under the surface.

'Oh,' he said, awkwardly putting the cup down on the table. 'They've already started building the road. We need to get moving a bit quicker than that.'

'Ah,' said Ian, stroking his stubbly chin. 'Well, you could do something smaller, I guess. Get a few of us into the houses. Rely on squatter's rights.'

'Sounds good,' said George.

'What's this about?' asked Kaz, coming over.

'George is organising a protest,' Ian told her.

'About this road they're building through Ashton Park.'

Kaz stared at George in wonder. 'I didn't have you as a Green,' she said.

'Well,' said George, 'I don't like labels. But we have to stop this road.'

Ian nodded but Kaz didn't seem so impressed. 'Why?'

'Huh?' said George.

'Why does it have to be stopped? They build roads all the time.'

George didn't know what to say. Of course he couldn't explain the real reason; that he wanted to help out a ghost.

'Exactly,' said Ian, and for an instant George thought he had read his thoughts. 'They're building them all the time,' Ian went on. 'That's why they've got to be stopped.'

Kaz grinned. 'All right,' she said. 'Count me in.'

'So when can we do this?' asked George. 'What do I need to do?'

'When are you free?' said Ian.

George considered. 'I'm off tomorrow. We could meet up to plan it out.'

Ian shook his head. 'What's to plan?' he said. 'We know where the thing's being built. We just need to rally support.'

'Right,' said George. 'And how—'

'I can get onto that,' said Ian. 'I know people. Radical email lists, stuff like that.'

George grinned. 'So when...?'

Ian and Kaz exchanged glances.

'You said you were free tomorrow,' said Ian. 'So tomorrow it is.'

Chapter
EIGHT

Mitchell didn't want to play board games.

Gemma had completed the Inspector Morse jigsaw, and then she and Annie were bored. So Annie had looked through the junk that Mitchell had once thought would transform the house into a home. She'd produced MB's Ghost Castle and The Vampire Game. They hadn't been that funny when Mitchell had bought them. Now they filled him with fury.

Because he couldn't understand why Gemma sat slumped there on the sofa. She didn't want to talk or go out or do anything; she was even worse than Annie. They'd told her that Lee, her son, might also be a ghost and that the house he haunted was at risk. And she just shrugged sadly like that was all she expected.

Mitchell wanted to shout at her. Why didn't she do something?

But Annie was just as bad. She liked having another ghost around – maybe it helped her feel normal. In fact, just as with Gilbert a few months before, it seemed to make her feel superior. A ghost with the clothes and quirks from years back meant Annie was the cool one.

No, Mitchell thought, that wasn't fair. There was something else between Annie and Gemma. They'd both been abused by the things that waited on the other side of the door. They'd both suffered the things that could never be spoken of, that even a hundred-year-old vampire like himself had barely glimpsed.

'Your turn,' Annie pouted.

Mitchell reached for the pair of dice and popped them into the plastic shaker. With his hand over the open end, he rattled the dice then scattered them onto the board.

'A two and a one!' Annie cried out, clapping her hands together. 'You'll never catch us up!'

Mitchell stared at the dog-eared board with its garish illustrations. Ghosts and vampires were just a joke to ordinary people. He couldn't see them making board games out of other afflictions. Or maybe there was a market in exactly that: garishly illustrated board games based on cancer or swine flu.

'Mitchell,' Annie told him. 'You have to move your pieces.'

He sighed. 'What's the point? You've vanquished me.'

'Vanquished,' smiled Gemma. 'That's a word.'

'You're both too good for this poor soldier,' said Mitchell grandly, knocking over his playing piece with one finger. 'I throw myself on your mercy.'

'You can't surrender!' wailed Annie. 'We have to get to the end.'

'And I,' said Mitchell, getting to his feet and grabbing his leather jacket, 'have to get to work.'

'It's not fair,' said Annie. 'We never finish a game.'

'Life's not fair,' Gemma told her. 'Let him go.'

'It's more a numb disappointment,' Mitchell agreed. 'You're well out of it.'

Annie poked her tongue out at him, then wrapped her arms around her knees as she always did when she didn't get her way.

'I'll be back around ten,' Mitchell told them. 'We'll know what George is planning by then. Don't you worry, Gemma. We'll sort things out for your son.'

Gemma didn't seem to hear him, too busy packing up the game.

'Well,' said Mitchell, annoyed. 'Don't do anything I wouldn't.'

Neither Annie nor Gemma acknowledged him. He sighed, feeling like he'd failed them. And also angry that they'd made him feel like he'd failed. He escaped into the daylight, leaving them at the coffee table, letting the day pass them by.

He considered the problem as he made his way to work. Annie didn't like going outside at the best of times at the moment, but just the previous day she and Gemma had gone to the park. It had looked as if Gemma might be good news, bringing Annie out of herself again. But now they were both hiding out in the living room – ironically – and nothing would elicit a response.

Not even the potential risk to Gemma's son.

Perhaps Mitchell and George needed to head down to Bryn Road and see the house for themselves. If the street was being demolished he supposed no one would mind them having a nose around. Anything of value would long since have been pinched. What harm could they do?

But Mitchell also didn't like the idea of playing detective quite so openly. He was a vampire, he was meant to lurk in the shadows. There had been a time when he'd thought it best to be as visible as he could, opening the house to the neighbours and sharing out beer and his DVDs. That hadn't exactly worked out.

So no, there had to be a better way to make contact with Gemma's son. He wondered what the boy would be like. He'd have been born in 1981, so what would he have been into? Mitchell wracked his brain, trying to recall the details from the long clutter of his life. Stuff from the early 1990s to appeal to a 10-year-old boy. Pokémon and the *Star Wars* prequels – were those the right sort of thing?

Or maybe he was into sport. Mitchell would have to ask Gemma if Lee had supported a team. Then he could Google the history and bluff his way with the rest. Mitchell had a knack for talking to anyone, for putting them in his thrall.

But what would he say to some gawky teenager who'd been hanging around unnoticed for the last ten years? That didn't exactly promise an easy conversation. He'd seen enough ghosts who'd gone without human contact so long that they'd lost the ability to speak. They would drag around behind the living, drawn to their warmth and vitality. But they would never get close, just lurk in the darkness, staring and forlorn.

A thought struck Mitchell and he laughed to himself, startling a woman and child coming the other way up the pavement. He grinned at them and the woman despite herself grinned back. Mitchell reached in his pockets for a cigarette, delighted.

He had seen that exact ghostly, forlorn expression just the day before. Mitchell didn't believe in coincidence. A gawky, black teenager had hidden in the darkness, watching the almost-dead of Intensive Care. The kid had stared at him, surprised to be seen, then vanished into the air.

He was sure now that it had been Gemma's son, Lee.

George was waiting for him at the main entrance on Little Guinea Street.

Mitchell flicked away the stub of his cigarette as he approached.

'Hey,' he said. 'Waiting for me?'

'No,' said George, rubbing his hands together briskly to fight off the cold. 'I thought I'd have a smoke. Except everyone else seems to have given up so there's no one to borrow off.'

Mitchell offered George his open packet. George just stared at him over the top of his glasses. Mitchell shrugged.

'So,' he said. 'How are you getting along?'

George grinned at him. 'I've only organised a protest for tomorrow afternoon. Texts have been sent out and everything.'

'So what's the plan?' asked Mitchell.

'Just turn up,' said George. 'Everyone else gets texted an hour before we start. We meet at the end of Bryn Road at three, then walk up looking for suitable houses. Ones we can get into, ones that have running water if we can.'

'We're moving in?' asked Mitchell, hardly enthralled by the prospect.

'We're not,' George told him. 'But Ian and his mates will. They've done this stuff before. The council can't just drag them out of the buildings, they have to get some kind of permission from a court. And that might buy us weeks.'

'Very good,' said Mitchell, grinning. 'I knew you could do it. Don't think Annie and Gemma believed me, but I said you could.'

'Yeah!' agreed George. Then he did one of his patented double-takes. 'What did Annie and Gemma say?'

'Never mind,' said Mitchell, taking George by the arm and leading him into the hospital. 'You've proven them wrong anyway. Well done.'

George took the compliment but tried to free his arm from Mitchell's. They squabbled and slapped at each other as they made their way through the double-doors. Sarah on reception looked up as they came in and grinned.

Mitchell and George immediately stopped fooling about. They each folded their arms, held their heads high with serious expressions, and both headed off in different directions.

Sarah leaned across her desk to watch them go, with a sigh.

When Mitchell had a moment, he took himself upstairs and into Intensive Care. He thrilled at the prospect as he leapt up the stairs and along the corridor, but the moment he passed into the low-lit ward, he had to stop in his tracks.

The machines were working their eerie magic on the dozen bodies round the room. Lights flickered, breath hissed mechanically – the only signs of life. Mitchell fought the instinctive urge to turn and run. This place got right under his skin.

'Um,' he called out. 'Hello?' He ventured forward, eyes fast adjusting to the gloom.

A balding man in his early 30s looked up from beside one of the beds. He clutched the hand of the sleeping old woman there, as if afraid it might fall off. Mitchell smiled at the man, a gesture of support. The man quickly lowered his eyes back down to the old woman's hand. Mitchell continued down the aisle of sleeping bodies.

'Oh,' said a voice ahead of him. Kaz got up from her desk and started towards him.

Mitchell smiled. Kaz was much better than Gail. Gail would never let him have a look round. He tried to think of excuses that didn't involve searching for a ghost.

'You heard,' said Kaz.

Mitchell didn't know what she was talking about, but he saw her glance over his shoulder at the row of beds. One of the beds stood empty. The one, the day before, where Mr Wright had slept.

'He went about eleven last night,' said Kaz. 'Peaceful. Must have had good karma.'

Mitchell nodded. 'And his wife?'

'What do you think?' said Kaz. 'I got her a cup of tea. You know he used to be a porter here?'

'Yeah,' said Mitchell.

'Glimpse of your future,' said Kaz. 'If you don't keep your nose clean.'

'What do you mean?' asked Mitchell.

'Oh,' said Kaz. 'I asked round. Mr Wright left under a bit of a cloud. Was on the hospital computers when no one else was looking.'

Mitchell took a moment to get what she was implying. 'He was looking at porn?'

'Not that he ever admitted. And no one really wanted to hear him confess. They looked the other way. That's how Gail says phallocentric ideology perpetuates itself.'

'She's probably onto something there,' said Mitchell. 'So what happened?'

'They let him take early retirement.'

Mitchell stared at the empty bed. He wondered what – and how much – Mrs Wright had known, or suspected. She'd told Mitchell her husband had told her everything, and then she'd stuck with him to the end. Mitchell had liked her in that short time they'd spent together in the lift. Now he wished he'd been able to do more than just call her a cab.

Then Mitchell felt a prickle run through him, a sixth sense that he was being watched. He glanced over at the balding man in the tweed jacket, who quickly lowered his head. Mitchell watched him but the man didn't look up again. He clutched the hand of the old woman lying in front of him, an agonised look on his face.

'Mr Foot,' Kaz told him. 'Not seen him before yesterday, but his auntie's been here for months. He's been devoted today, though. Just sits there holding her hand.' She grinned. 'Don't think he'll need an escort. You can go if you want.'

Mitchell turned back to Kaz. 'No,' he said. 'Er, I wanted a word with you anyway.'

Kaz regarded him carefully. 'Me,' she said.

'Yeah,' said Mitchell. 'I mean. About Gail. We didn't hit it off yesterday. And then I was talking to George. You know George?'

'Who doesn't know George?' said Kaz. 'You two live together, don't you?'

'Yeah,' said Mitchell. 'We go way back. Anyway, he said—' He stopped, realising what Kaz really meant. She thought he and George were an item – and she wasn't the first to think that. What had George said? Had he meant to say it? Mitchell couldn't wait to find out.

But for the moment it suited Mitchell to play along. Being gay would immediately scupper Gail's accusation of the previous day.

'He said,' Mitchell told her, 'that you knew about us. And that I should come and see you.'

'You want me to tell Gail she got it wrong about your womanising,' Kaz told him.

'Well,' said Mitchell. 'Yeah.'

'I saw George earlier today, too,' she said. 'I didn't understand about you two.'

'That's all right,' said Mitchell. 'Not many people do.'

'You've got an open relationship,' she said. 'You see who you want to. Women as well.'

Mitchell looked her in the eye. 'I'm very supportive of George,' he said piously.

'And you're going to support him in his thing?' said Kaz.

'His road protest?' said Mitchell. Kaz had braids and earrings, he reasoned. She'd be into that sort of stuff. 'Oh yeah, sure. It's important.'

Kaz laughed. 'Yes, it is.' She leant forward, conspiratorially. 'But I meant the other thing.'

'Oh,' said Mitchell, with heavy emphasis. 'That. Sure. I support him in everything. Well, I try to.' He had no idea what she meant.

'Gail,' said Kaz, 'is sort of the same. I want to go for it for all guns blazing, she says she's just being wary. But I think that cynicism can corrode the spirit.'

Mitchell scratched at one of his sideburns. 'I'm not cynical,' he said.

'That's what Gail says, too!' said Kaz. She laughed. 'Oh, you're really like her. And I almost believed all the things they said about you! You eating women alive!'

Mitchell screwed his face up in horror. 'I wouldn't know where to start!' He was enjoying himself.

'But you're all right with George...' She tailed off.

Kaz didn't seem the shy sort, thought Mitchell. She'd more likely blurt out something indelicate for the whole ward to hear. But now she seemed coy about whatever she'd got happening with George.

'It's all right,' he told her.

She toyed with her earrings. 'Gail and me,' she said. 'We both believe in freedom. I think it's good you'd support George in something like this.'

Mitchell stared at her. What was she on about? Did she fancy George? Had Gail given permission for Kaz to sleep with him? He wanted to laugh, but instead he said, 'George isn't like other guys.'

Kaz took his hands in hers. 'I knew you'd understand,' she said, all hostility forgotten. 'I could see it in your aura. And we'll support each other, won't we? We'll share whatever happens. It'll be a good experience.'

'Of course it will,' Mitchell told her. George owed him for this. 'We're all friends now.'

Kaz nodded. 'Friends,' she said. Then she glanced round the ward – at balding Mr Foot still clutching the old woman's hand, and at the rest of the bodies. She looked back at Mitchell and grinned nervously.

'Would you watch the ward for five minutes?'

Mitchell shrugged. 'Sure, we're friends.'

Kaz nodded, her earrings jangling. 'Good,' she said. 'I'm desperate, and the Ladies is on the next floor.'

She hurried off, leaving the Intensive Care Unit in Mitchell's hands.

'Is there anything the boys can't eat?' asked Gemma as she rifled through the cupboards.

'Those two will eat everything,' Annie grinned. She stood in the doorway of the kitchen watching Gemma turn everything out. She and Gemma had already done the washing up. They'd vacuumed, they'd dusted and now they were working their way through all the cupboards and drawers.

Gemma was doing most of the work, but she'd give Annie small jobs to do. Annie had gone through the cutlery drawer, making sure everything in it was clean. She'd taken down the noticeboard and weeded through the leaflets and scraps of paper pinned to it, binning anything out of date. It felt good to be doing something, anything.

'I mean,' said Gemma, emerging from the cupboard with an empty box of cereal. 'They both have their *conditions*. Is there anything I should avoid?'

Annie considered. 'You mean like garlic and holy water?'

'Do they affect Mitchell?' said Gemma. 'I wouldn't want to hurt him.'

'Mitchell loves garlic,' said Annie. 'He loves all kinds of spicy food. I think he lived in India once.'

'That's good,' said Gemma, returning to the cupboard.

'George won't eat pork sometimes, when he remembers,' said Annie. 'And he can't eat marzipan, either.'

Gemma withdrew from the cupboard again. 'Marzipan?' she said, eyes wide. 'The almonds make him sick?'

'No,' said Annie. 'He just doesn't like it very much. I think his mum used to make a lot of cakes.'

Gemma sighed. Annie laughed. 'You almost look disappointed.'

Gemma laughed. 'I am! Just imagine. A werewolf, and done for by marzipan.'

'That wouldn't make a very good movie,' said Annie.

'No,' said Gemma. 'Ah well. I'll do them something spicy tonight. I know just the thing.'

'Great,' said Annie. 'What are we doing?'

Gemma's smile faltered. 'We?' she said.

'Yeah,' said Annie. 'Me and you.'

Gemma shrugged. 'Well if you want to,' she said.

'That's all right, isn't it?' said Annie. 'You don't mind?'

'No,' said Gemma. 'And it's good you want to help. I said a bit of housework would make us feel better.'

Annie stared at her. 'It was my idea.'

Gemma sighed. 'Well it was a good idea, whoever's it was,' she said as she turned her back on Annie to get on with the cupboard.

Annie watched her, feeling stupid and selfish. 'I didn't mean...' she said, sadly.

'I know,' said Gemma from inside the cupboard. 'I know.'

But Annie felt scarred by the disappointment in her voice.

First, Mitchell went over to the desk and rummaged around for a piece of paper and a pen. Mr Foot, the balding man sat by the sleeping old woman, looked up at him, grief written on his face. Mitchell gave him a reassuring smile and got on with his work.

He found a spiral-bound notebook and flipped to a blank page. In blue biro he wrote five words: *Lee, I can help you.*

Mitchell studied the words for a moment, considering other options. Then he dropped the pen. It clattered on the desk as he tore the page from the notebook.

Mr Foot was watching him when Mitchell looked up. Mitchell smiled at him, then made a point of reading the blank side of the page from the notebook. As he read the words that weren't there, Mitchell turned a full circle, sharing his message to Lee with the whole ward.

Then Mitchell waited.

Nothing. If Lee had seen him, he wasn't coming forward. Still holding the page so that anyone else could read it, Mitchell began to walk back up the ward.

He stopped at each of the bodies, gazing over their sleeping forms. The machines ticked and twitched, maintaining them.

Mr Wright's bed lay empty and Mitchell found himself drawn to it. Soon there'd be some other poor soul under the sheet and blanket, strapped up to the machines. The twittering lights marked time until the sleeper awoke or just slipped away. Mitchell had only a cursory knowledge of the ways these things worked. As a porter passing through the wards there seemed no rhyme or reason, no rule for who lived and who died. There were obvious things – obesity and smoking both cut down your chances – but mostly it seemed life got decided on the flick of a coin.

In the next bed lay Rebecca Hywel-Jones, kept alive artificially for all of a decade. Born 14 July 1981. It seemed such a recent date, Mitchell could almost remember what he'd been doing. Probably sat in watching telly, feeling sorry for himself.

If he hadn't known her age, he might have guessed anywhere between 20 and 40, Mitchell thought. Her skin seemed tanned, her teeth gleamed brilliant white where they could be seen through her barely parted lips. Mitchell glanced at Mr Foot to check he wasn't looking, then wiped his finger down Rebecca's cheek to check she wasn't wearing make-up. No, it seemed the coma or the medication had given the girl a healthy glow.

Her life had hardly started and here she was, sleeping through it. He wondered what had happened to her in 1999 –

Mitchell must have said something because Mr Foot looked up. They stared at each other, Mitchell in shock and Mr Foot in surprise. Then Mitchell hurried back to Kaz's desk. Mr Wright had lost his job for using one of the computers, and Mitchell knew he'd be in hot water if anyone caught him doing the same. But this couldn't wait, he had to risk it.

He plonked himself down on the swivel chair

in front of her computer and began hammering at the keyboard. The hospital database asked for a password. Mitchell knew at least half a dozen. Soon he had the records up for Rebecca Hywel-Jones.

The dates couldn't be a coincidence. Born the same year as Gemma's son Lee, and she had fallen into a coma the same year Lee and Gemma had died. Then Mitchell had spotted Lee hanging round the ward where she slept. Had Lee known her before he'd died? Had they been sweethearts or something? Was that the connection?

Mitchell scanned through the details. She'd been brought into A&E complaining of headaches and sickness. The staff thought she'd been drinking but it soon proved to be something else. Symptoms included vomiting, convulsions and haemorrhage. They'd still been doing tests when she'd lapsed into the coma. It looked like she'd had a bad reaction to some kind of amphetamine.

Poor kid, thought Mitchell. A night out on Ecstasy aged 18, and then in here ever since.

Had Lee known her? Had he given her the drugs, or been there when it happened? That might explain why he'd killed himself and then hung round ever since. Though, Mitchell had to admit, he didn't seem to be on the ward now.

He reached for the mouse, clicking print on the file. As the pages licked out of the printer, Mitchell looked over the desk. Kaz would be back any moment. He needed to hide the print-out from her.

This was worse than porn: he knew he was on the trail of something hidden for years.

There were depressingly few pages for a girl who'd been on the ward for ten years. Mitchell gathered them from the print tray and rolled them round his left forearm. It proved easy enough to hide them under the sleeve of his scrubs, the end of the pages tucked in under his watchstrap to keep them secure.

Pleased with this perfect crime, Mitchell logged out of the database and left the desk as he had found it. He made his way back up the ward, ready to meet Kaz in the doorway.

Mr Foot watched him. Mitchell didn't register that he'd seen, just kept on walking forward. But as he made his way up the aisle of beds, he could feel Mr Foot watching.

Mitchell took a breath, let his predator instincts reach out. He could hear Mr Foot's heart hammering fast inside his ribcage. Mitchell could almost taste the man's clammy sweat and fear. He'd not tasted blood for two days now – since the new administrator had arrived – and this man was giving off all the signals of prey.

Kaz appeared in the doorway, hurrying towards him.

Mitchell blinked away the blackness in his eyes and smiled at her.

'Thanks,' she told him as she got close, breathless from running up the stairs. He could hear her heart and the blood coursing through her. He could easily snap her neck.

'No problem,' he said, nonchalantly putting the arm with the concealed pages behind his back. 'Best be off. People are watching.'

'Yeah,' said Kaz. 'See you at the protest.'

'Yeah,' said Mitchell. 'See you then.'

He let her go back to the desk, watching to make sure he'd left everything in order. She didn't seem to find anything amiss.

Mitchell turned to go. And found Mr Foot staring at him, clutching the old woman's hand.

Mitchell glanced at Kaz, then back at Mr Foot. The man was positively trembling. Mitchell grinned. 'Can I help you?' he asked.

The man tried to smile but it came out as a grimace. He clung on to the old woman's hand.

Mitchell looked down on Mr Foot's face, then looked over the sleeping old woman beside him. The name on the board said Barbara Mumbles, and she looked nothing like Mr Foot. Mr Foot might have been handsome until quite recently, but was now passing well into the indignities of middle age.

'She's not a relative,' said Mitchell, glancing between the two faces. He spoke softly, so Kaz wouldn't hear. He hoped instead that if she looked up it would seem like Mitchell was offering condolence.

'No,' said Mr Foot. 'Not a relative. More a, uh, friend.'

'But you do know who she is,' said Mitchell.

'Oh yes,' said Mr Foot. 'Barbara Mumbles. Born 28 July 1941!' He grinned up at Mitchell, like he deserved a prize.

'You could just have read that from the sign,' said Mitchell. 'What else can you tell me about her?'

Mr Foot looked at Barbara Mumbles sleeping on the bed, then at the sign above her. His whole body sagged, Barbara's fingers slipping from his. She lay there, not even aware of him.

'All right,' said Mr Foot, not even looking up at Mitchell. 'You got me.'

Mitchell almost wanted to laugh. 'And who are you really, Mr Foot?'

'Gavin,' said the man. 'Gavin Foot. That really is my name. I'm freelance for the *Daily Press*.'

'A journalist,' said Mitchell. 'What's the story?'

Gavin Foot looked up at him meekly. 'Would you believe,' he asked, 'ghosts?'

Chapter

NINE

'We can't talk here,' Mitchell told Gavin Foot.

Gavin nodded, understanding the implicit message – that Mitchell had something to tell him. He glanced up the Intensive Care ward to where Kaz sat at the desk. She seemed to be reading a battered old paperback.

'Where?' Gavin asked Mitchell.

Mitchell considered. 'Give me a minute.' He headed back over to Kaz. 'Hey!' he said as he got close.

She looked up, surprised by the noise. Intensive Care usually sat in respectful silence, like a church.

'Mr Foot could do with a cup of tea,' Mitchell told her. 'I'll show him the canteen.'

Kaz stared at him for a moment. 'He's grieving,' she said.

Mitchell smiled. She thought he'd made a pass at Gavin. Well, that was better than suspecting anything else.

'A cup of tea,' Mitchell insisted. 'That's all. He looks like he could do with it.'

Kaz sighed. 'Haven't you got anything better to do?'

'Oh, go on, I covered for you.'

'I'm not your boss,' she told him. But that wasn't the point. Mitchell needed someone to vouch for him, just in case anyone asked questions. Kaz wouldn't just say he'd gone to the canteen; she'd confirm Gavin Foot needed taking. She owed him that much, at least.

Mitchell led Gavin downstairs and through the warren of corridors to the canteen. The hospital had been expanded and adapted for decades, new wards and treatment rooms bolted on wherever there was space. Even with the signs everywhere, it took time to get to know your way round, the organic development more like a body than a building. Mitchell could see Gavin trying to remember the route. But they were on Mitchell's territory now.

'Hey,' said George, appearing from one of the cupboards, laden with freshly cleaned blankets in their cellophane wrappers.

'Sorry,' Mitchell told him. 'Can't stop.'

He pushed on, Gavin almost having to jog to keep up.

The canteen was empty, just as Mitchell had

hoped. The guy behind the counter didn't notice them at first, too engrossed in his copy of *The Mirror*. Gavin seized his chance and asked Mitchell what he wanted.

'Tea,' said Mitchell.

Gavin chose a coffee and a Twix for himself, and asked for a receipt. The guy behind the counter stared back at Gavin as if he were speaking a different language.

'Not to worry,' said Gavin quickly, handing over the £3.10. 'They don't like us claiming expenses, anyway.'

Mitchell didn't need Gavin telling everyone what he did for a living. Talking to journalists could be a disciplinary offence for anyone who worked in the hospital. Mitchell steered Gavin away from the counter. 'You get a table,' he said.

'There's no one else here,' said Gavin. 'We can sit anywhere we like.'

'Yeah, but get a table by the window,' said Mitchell. 'We won't be disturbed over there.'

Gavin looked across the tables and chairs to the window at the far end of the canteen. He nodded, eyes narrowed slyly. 'Understood,' he said, as if they were secret agents, and made his way across the room.

The guy behind the counter raised his eyebrows at Mitchell.

'Yeah,' said Mitchell. 'He's all right, really. Just not dealing with his aunt's treatment that well. Nurse asked me to get him out of their hair for a bit. Can you make sure people give us some space?'

The guy behind the counter nodded – he, too, doubled as an occasional therapist in this job. He gathered the tea and coffee and Twix and slid them over to Mitchell.

'Good luck,' he said.

'Cheers,' said Mitchell, balancing the Twix on top of the coffee and carrying everything over to Gavin.

The table looked out onto a narrow balcony, and the rain and the main road beyond. It hardly counted as a view, but once inside the labyrinth and bustle of the hospital you could forget the outside world existed. This window gave a tantalising glimpse.

'So,' said Mitchell. 'Ghosts.'

Gavin nodded, unwrapping his Twix. Resting it on the coffee had melted the chocolate. 'I know how it sounds,' he said, struggling now with chocolaty fingers. 'But we had more than a couple of tip-offs in the last few weeks. The sort of stuff that doesn't make any sense.'

Mitchell nodded. 'There's a new regime,' he said carefully.

'Yeah,' said Gavin. 'They're asking the same questions I am. Paperwork disappearing. Documents that should have been copied and sent on, but it's like they never existed.'

Mitchell considered. It was everything that he'd feared. The press had got their first hint of what really went on in the hospital. Gavin was five foot four, he guessed, and a bullishly built little man. He'd probably been pretty good-looking in his twenties, had maybe played sport – perhaps rugby. But now he was filling out and balding, fast hitting middle age. You could see he resented it, and his place in this world. Getting old, and knowing it. Realising that he still hadn't made his mark on the world. A man with something to prove.

That, Mitchell knew, made him dangerous.

'You're not denying it,' said Gavin.

'You think there's some kind of conspiracy?' laughed Mitchell. But that was the wrong way to play the situation. Gavin's expression hardened against him.

'There's something,' Gavin said. 'And I'm going to find out what it is.'

'It could just be accidental,' said Mitchell with more interest. 'Files go missing sometimes.'

'These are repeated incidents,' said Gavin. 'Going back months, maybe years.'

Mitchell had known a few journalists in his time. The old-school lot had a code of honour about good stories being hard work. This guy, on a local paper, had that same drive. The more a story didn't make sense the better it would ultimately be when he unravelled it.

'You said ghosts,' said Mitchell, but without the mocking tone he'd used before. He just wanted to provoke Gavin, get him to share what he knew.

'It might as well be,' said Gavin. 'People doing things here that no one else sees. It's like they're clearing up behind everyone else. Vanishing anything illicit.'

'A conspiracy,' said Mitchell.

Gavin smiled. 'One of my tutors at Central Lancashire had a thing about conspiracies. You don't put anything down to conspiracy that can be put down to incompetence.'

Mitchell grinned. 'Yeah, well, in this place…'

'It's not incompetent,' said Gavin. 'It's far too neat. There's a pattern to it.'

'You got any proof?' Mitchell asked.

Gavin smiled. 'The same proof as you.' He reached out a hand and pointed at Mitchell's sleeve. The sleeve in which Mitchell had stowed the pages he'd printed out.

Gavin glanced round to ensure no one else could hear. They were alone in the canteen but for the guy behind the counter, who remained caught up in his paper. Even so, Gavin whispered.

'Rebecca Hywel-Jones,' he said.

There seemed no point in denying it, so Mitchell nodded his head.

'Admitted on the fourth of September, 1999. She'd taken some kind of amphetamine, probably home-made but definitely not very well. Been in a coma ever since.'

Again Mitchell nodded.

Gavin smiled, glad he'd got something Mitchell

didn't know. 'But who else was with her?' he asked. When Mitchell didn't answer, he added, 'Check the file you printed out.'

Carefully, Mitchell eased the pages from his sleeve and unrolled them. He scanned through the details. Yes, she'd been brought in on the fourth of September, and she had tested positive for amphetamines. There were details of the tests done, of who she'd been seen by, the various administration brackets she'd come under. Mitchell scoured the document for clues, but he couldn't see anything out of order.

'Two things,' Gavin told him when Mitchell sat back, defeated. And Mitchell could see it: Gavin knew he was good at his job, and needed someone else to notice. He craved that acknowledgement, he'd do anything. There was no way he'd keep what he discovered silent.

'Go on,' said Mitchell, fearing for the man's life. If he looked too hard, he'd meet the vampires. And they wouldn't take him for a coffee and a Twix.

'First,' said Gavin. 'She's been on the same ward for ten years.'

Mitchell looked down at the notes. There was no word of where Rebecca had spent her time. Even if she'd never been moved, there should have been some mention. There were places that specialised in long-term care, places that would have been better for her. Oh, there were exceptions, but those exceptions should have been listed in her file.

'And second?' he asked.

'Secondly,' Gavin said, emphasising the last syllable like Mitchell had made some horrendous grammatical error. 'There's no mention of who else she came in with.'

Again, Mitchell looked down at the notes. There was no mention of anyone else, just a contact number for Rebecca's mum, now living somewhere in France. Poor woman, thought Mitchell, trying to get on with her life and never able to run far enough away. Something had happened to that woman's daughter, something never explained. And Gavin was hard on the heels of the mystery.

'Who?' Mitchell asked him.

'It's not in her notes,' said Gavin. 'I looked it up in my own paper, but there's no story on the database, either.'

'You didn't cover it?'

Gavin shook his head sadly. 'It's the sort of thing we would. Teenage coma has emotional cachet with our readers.' He almost spat the words, no friend of a journalism run by buzz words and demographics.

'So maybe someone leant on the paper at the time,' said Mitchell.

'Or has had it removed from the database since,' said Gavin. He beamed. 'I went to the archive and looked through the physical copies.'

'And?'

'A story, printed two days later. Quotes from the mother of one of the other victims.'

Gavin withdrew a Moleskine notebook from the

pocket of his tweed jacket. He pinged off the elastic and leafed through the pages until he found what he needed. Mitchell took the notebook from him and examined the precise handwriting.

There were four names listed. Two, Thomas Ho and Barry Jones, had died that night. Chantell Roy – 'without a second e', Gavin's note said – and Rebecca Hywel-Jones had both been put in Intensive Care.

'They all came in on the same night,' said Gavin. 'They'd all taken the same drug. Chantell Roy died just this last Sunday. A night later – two nights ago – someone got into my paper's database and deleted the story.'

Mitchell nodded, slowly. Decades of painstaking effort to stay hidden, and the vampires were getting sloppy. 'What did she die of?' he said, already suspecting the answer. There'd be two small holes in her neck.

But Gavin shrugged. 'There's not much in her notes.'

Mitchell nodded. 'I can ask round.'

'Don't take any risks for this,' Gavin told him. 'You could lose your job.'

Mitchell smiled. 'I can ask round gently. See what people know. Better than you stumbling about, holding some old lady's hand.'

Gavin flushed. 'I didn't know how else to—'

'Hey,' said Mitchell. 'That was smart.'

As he'd hoped, the compliment worked, Gavin sat up straighter, beaming.

151

'And,' said Mitchell with a grin, 'the old love probably liked the attention.'

Gavin grinned back. Yeah, thought Mitchell, they were partners now. Gavin would tell him anything.

'So,' he asked, swigging his tea, making it seem a casual question. 'What put you on to this?'

Gavin took a breath. 'Again,' he said. 'Ghosts.'

'Ghosts,' said Mitchell, intrigued.

'Someone left a card on the news editor's desk this morning,' said Gavin. 'The four kids' names, and the fact that someone had messed with their files. She passed it to me.'

'But no one saw who left the card,' said Mitchell.

'That's the thing,' Gavin told him. 'It wasn't posted, it was just there. Someone came into the building.'

'Or,' said Mitchell, 'was already there. But invisible.'

'Yeah,' said Gavin. 'So it must have been someone I work with. That happens. The story can be too close to home, or involve someone you know. So you tip off one of the other reporters. That's what the news editor said.'

'She must be right,' Mitchell agreed. But he'd got his own ideas.

Gavin might not know it, but he really was on the trail of a ghost.

Kaz confirmed what Gavin had said. A girl called Chantell – without the second 'e' – Roy had died just that Sunday evening. But there'd not been anything strange about it, and no marks on her neck.

'Sometimes they just fade away,' Kaz explained. 'Her family came in when we called them. I think it was a bit of a relief. Now they can all move on.'

Mitchell nodded. He wanted a look at Chantell's file, but that would have to wait.

'Which was her spot?' he asked, just making conversation.

Kaz pointed to the empty bed which had briefly been occupied by Mr Wright. 'There,' she said.

Mitchell nodded. 'She must have been about the same age as the girl in the next one along.'

Kaz looked at him puzzled. 'Hardly a girl; she's 28.'

'And so was Chantell,' said Mitchell.

'I guess,' sighed Kaz, playing with the earrings in one ear. 'They can't have known each other, though.'

'No?' asked Mitchell, again playing it casual.

'No,' said Kaz. 'How could they? It would have been in their notes.'

'Gemma?' called Annie. She wrapped her silver cardigan round herself, tightly, as if it could protect her from the fear. There was no answer.

Annie edged into the living room. The games were neatly stacked in their boxes on the table. The magazines had been tidied away. It all looked spick and span, except there was no sign of Gemma.

'Hello?' Annie called out, her voice wavering.

Had *they* come for her? Had they been in the house?

'Hello, dear,' said Gemma, right behind her.

Annie wheeled round like she'd been hit by a thunderbolt. 'Where've you been?' she demanded.

Gemma stood tall and broad-shouldered, a curious look on her face. Like she found Annie amusing but not really worth her attention.

'I finished in the kitchen,' she said.

'But I looked,' said Annie. 'You weren't there.'

'You can't have been looking hard enough,' Gemma chided. 'I was there the whole time.' She reached out, took Annie's hand. 'What is it, dear? What's got you like this?'

Annie let herself be led to the leather sofa, her small hand in both of Gemma's.

'I just thought,' Annie said meekly, 'they might have come for you. You know. Through a door.'

Gemma nodded, taking this seriously. Annie was so grateful she could have wept. 'They might do,' said Gemma. 'They might do. But they haven't come for me yet.'

'I hate the waiting,' said Annie. 'Like we just have to sit around till they come and get us.' She grinned at Gemma. 'Let's go out. We deserve it. We cleaned the whole house.'

'Where would we go?' said Gemma.

'Anywhere,' said Annie. 'To the park. Or the zoo! I haven't been to the zoo since I died.'

Gemma nodded slowly, but Annie could see she didn't like the prospect.

'What?' Annie asked.

'I know you want to do something,' said Gemma. 'But it's evening now. The zoo will be closed.'

'That doesn't matter to us!'

Gemma smiled. 'You don't want to exhaust yourself,' she said.

Annie bristled. She wanted to tell Gemma about taking on the legion of vampires, about how she'd refused to walk through her own door. But that seemed a lifetime ago now. That tough Annie had melted away into the air. This Annie couldn't even keep doing a job in the local pub. And Gemma was right – Annie did feel tired.

'I could almost go to bed,' she told Gemma.

Gemma smiled. 'Sometimes the best thing is to do nothing at all and not work yourself up. Your boys are working on why I'm here. You don't want to get in their way.'

'No,' Annie agreed, 'but—'

'We're safe here,' said Gemma, glancing round the living room. 'But outside we're exposed.'

Annie's eyes opened wide. 'What's out there?' she asked.

Gemma opened her mouth to tell her, then looked quickly away. 'You don't need to know,' she said. 'You've just got to trust me.' She turned back, gazing into Annie's eyes. Again, she took Annie's hands in hers. 'You do trust me, don't you?'

Annie stared back. She wanted to nod, but she couldn't move her head. 'Yes,' she managed to say.

'I *need* you to trust me,' said Gemma. 'It's all I got holding me together.'

'I trust you,' Annie assured her. She had only glimpsed whatever phantoms haunted Gemma. Gemma had endured them for a decade and knew just what they could do.

'OK,' said Gemma gratefully. 'OK.' She reached for the stack of board games again. 'So,' she said. 'A game. And then the boys will be back home and their tea will be waiting.'

As Gemma opened the box and unpacked the pieces, Annie glanced up at the window on the far side of the door. Pale light broke through the frosted glass, a hint of the damp, cold world outside. For a moment Annie had an urge to run out into it, to keep running, to be free.

Then she turned back to the board game Gemma was assembling. No, she told herself, this was better. This was safe.

'Mitchell,' sneered Albert. 'I hear you wanted a word.'

He kicked aside the *wet floor* sign and marched across Mitchell's pristine floor, leaving muddy footprints. Albert had been nobody back when Herrick ran Bristol's vampires; now he was one of those jostling to replace him. Albert was trying to act like he'd already taken charge.

Mitchell leant on the handle of his mop, wiping the sweat from his forehead with the back of his hand. 'Hey,' he said. 'You didn't need to rush.'

Albert stood before him, in his immaculate black suit and long coat, hair greased to perfection. Yet no matter how much money he spent on clothes and lotions, Albert would always look like what he was: a thug in pinstripe. He never looked comfortable, he could never relax. It was like he was waiting for someone to point him out as a fraud.

Which didn't work when the whole raison d'être of the vampires was to pass unnoticed. Not that Albert would have understood the term.

He smiled at Mitchell. 'I didn't rush,' he said.

'That's OK,' said Mitchell, who resumed mopping the floor, talking to Albert over his shoulder. 'I just meant, it wasn't urgent.'

He continued mopping, taking his time, as if Albert wasn't there. It was child's play to rile him, Mitchell knew. A long time ago they'd fought over which of them had been Herrick's favourite. Even when Mitchell had gone rogue, swearing off blood and breaking with everyone, Herrick had still liked him best. Albert might be useful as a blunt instrument, but he'd never been very smart. And Herrick liked them smart.

'Nevertheless,' said Albert, at length. 'Here I am.'

'Oh yeah,' said Mitchell, still mopping.

'Is it the new administrator?' Albert teased. 'Are you worried about keeping your job?' Then the humour was gone from his voice. 'We're watching this Dr McGough.'

'It's not him,' said Mitchell. 'It's just I noticed a thing. Nothing much. These two girls in a coma. Their records have been changed.'

Albert nodded slowly. 'You mean the records don't mention the holes they've got in their necks?'

Mitchell grinned. 'I don't think they're ours. The one I saw hadn't been bitten.'

Albert folded his arms. 'So why would we be changing the records?'

'That's what I wanted to know,' said Mitchell. 'It's not urgent. Just puzzling.'

'We don't mess around,' Albert told him. 'We only change what we need to. Herrick liked the soft touch.'

'You'd know about that,' said Mitchell.

Albert took a step forward, ready to punch him. Mitchell spun the mop deftly in his hands, brandishing it as a weapon. Albert struck out and Mitchell wrapped him hard across the knuckles.

'Ow!' said Albert. 'There's no need for that!'

'Don't like it when I'm crowded,' said Mitchell.

Albert sucked on his knuckles. 'What's this about?'

'You don't know anything about it?'

'It's not us.'

Mitchell didn't trust him – either to know in the first place, or to say if he did. 'You seem pretty sure.'

'I said. We don't mess with anything we don't have to. Do you think Herrick would have allowed it?'

Mitchell grinned. That was different. If Herrick had made them keep a low profile, Mitchell could believe Albert making the vampires stick to it even now. The vampires were floundering without a leader – whatever Albert might think about his having stepped up to take Herrick's place. They were letting things slip, they were almost being spotted, but they were still trying to stick to the old rules.

'All right,' he said. 'I believe you.'

'This about the journalist?' said Albert.

Mitchell didn't look up at him, just kept mopping the floor. 'The what?' he said.

'Gavin Foot,' said Albert. 'You and him had tea. How sweet. But he's been asking a lot of questions, hasn't he?'

Mitchell stepped forward. 'Leave him alone.'

Albert smiled. 'Is that a threat?'

Mitchell scowled. 'You want to find out?'

Albert stared at him, neither man yielding ground. They didn't even blink. But Albert knew Mitchell of old – knew exactly what he was capable of. He stepped back.

'All right,' he said. 'He's yours.'

Mitchell nodded. 'You make sure everyone knows. Anything happens to him, I won't be happy.'

'Oh dear,' said Albert. 'We can't have that.' He

159

grinned at Mitchell. 'You know he can't print anything. It can't be allowed. For your sake as much as for ours. Have him if you want him. But you'll have to deal with him yourself.'

Mitchell stepped forward to say something, but turned at a noise behind him. A woman on a zimmer frame clattered through the door, slapping into his wet floor sign. Mitchell turned back to Albert, but Albert had gone. There was nothing more that could be said.

Mitchell ran over to help the old woman before she slipped on his shiny floor.

He couldn't wait for the end of his shift, so of course it dragged. Mitchell had corridors to clean, and then a patient had an accident in one of the bathrooms. That became his job, as well. To be fair, it turned out to be quite an accident: it must have taken some doing to smear the ceiling quite that thoroughly.

He carried on working after the end of his shift, then headed back up to Intensive Care. Kaz had gone home, and another nurse was on duty. Mitchell made a bit of small talk, only moderately chatting her up. Yes, she had a long night in front of her, she said, shackled to the desk. He gallantly offered to watch things while she nipped off for a cup of tea.

'What can happen in five minutes?' he said. 'This lot aren't going anywhere.'

Once she was gone it took him just a moment to log in to the system and find the notes for Chantell

Roy. He printed them out without looking at the details, already knowing what he would find. The pages were warm as he rolled them round his forearm with the pages about Rebecca Hywel-Jones that he'd printed out earlier. By the time the nurse came back, Mitchell had logged out and was perched on the end of the desk, looking innocent.

As he left the hospital, Mitchell found George waiting for him.

He seemed a little cross. 'Where have you been?' he demanded. 'I was starting to get worried!'

'Sweet, George, but I can look after myself,' replied Mitchell. 'Been looking into some stuff I think is connected to Gemma's son. Listen—'

'Oh yeah,' cut in George. 'You keep me waiting for hours then it's all about you.'

Mitchell reached into his leather jacket for a cigarette. 'All right,' he said. 'How was your day?'

'We've already got ten people saying they'll be there tomorrow,' pouted George.

Mitchell nodded. From his pocket he withdrew a business card, which he handed over. 'Give this guy a call. He might give you some coverage.'

'Gavin Foot,' George read from the card. 'Why are you talking to the *Daily Press*?'

Mitchell grinned. 'He's good. He's serious. Tell him you know me.'

'All right,' said George, pocketing the card. 'And you'll be there, as well.'

'What?' said Mitchell. 'Oh come on! That's not really me.'

'Or me!' said George. 'But you were the one who said we had to do something. You can't back out of it now.'

'All right,' said Mitchell wearily. 'I'll swap my shifts or something.'

They followed the road alongside the river, turning off to climb the steep hill up to Totterdown and their house. Neither spoke for a while, Mitchell smoking and George in a sulk.

'George,' said Mitchell at length, when he'd finished his cigarette. 'I said I'd be there.'

George sighed. 'It's not just that,' he said. 'Guffy's got this new thing now. I can't get into the isolation ward.'

'What?' said Mitchell, stopping in the street.

'Mossy said it was being shut off. So I went to have a look.'

'And?' Mitchell demanded. He could just see George blundering into what was clearly a trap.

'I didn't get that far,' George admitted. 'So many people asked where I was going. What am I going to do? I don't have anywhere else!'

Mitchell put his hand on George's shoulder. 'It's all right,' he said. 'We'll work something out.'

'What?' said George. 'There's nothing we can do.'

'We'll do something,' Mitchell insisted. 'Just leave it to me.'

George seemed to accept that, and they continued up the hill towards home. But Mitchell hadn't been convinced by his own words. He had no idea what they could do to get back into the isolation ward, or what other options they had.

As they stepped through the front door of the house, George and Mitchell were assailed by the most amazing aroma. Rich and sweet and spicy, it took Mitchell a moment to identify.

'Goat curry,' he said, heading through into the kitchen. 'I haven't had goat curry in years.'

Gemma beamed at him from where she tended the stove. The table was laid for four and a bottle of wine stood open. Annie got up from the table, grinning, as Mitchell came in. But there was something in her eyes, like she was putting on a brave face.

'What?' said Mitchell.

Annie ignored him, helping him out of his jacket. 'What time is this?' she chided. 'We expected you back more than an hour ago. Gemma's been going spare.'

'I have not,' said Gemma. 'Just worried you'd be hungry.'

She started serving up, so George and Mitchell quickly took their places. Annie fussed around them. She'd clearly wanted a word with Mitchell, or just to escape the kitchen. Now she had missed her chance.

'So where did you get the goat?' he asked.

'I went out and got it,' said Gemma.

'When?' said Annie, affronted. Gemma *had* vanished from the house.

'Earlier,' said Gemma. 'We needed ingredients. You were cleaning upstairs.'

'You cleaned the house,' said Mitchell. 'Brilliant. You know I'd been meaning to do that.'

'She went out,' Annie said to him. 'She went out without me.'

'I wanted it to be a surprise,' said Gemma. 'It's not a problem, is it?'

'Gemma's a grown woman,' said George. 'She can probably go to the shops on her own.'

'Of course she can,' said Annie.

But Mitchell saw the look in Annie's eyes. He knew the outside world terrified her at the moment, that it was she who couldn't go out on her own. She looked up at him, and he smiled back, trying to offer reassurance.

Annie sighed, knowing it was only a silly thing. 'Never mind,' she said.

'Pour the wine if you want to be useful,' Gemma told her.

To Mitchell's surprise, Annie did exactly as instructed. Dark wine glooped into the glass in front of him.

'Thank you,' he said. Annie beamed at him.

'When you're a waitress,' said Gemma, 'you hold the base of the bottle. Your thumb goes in the indentation.'

Wanting to oblige, Annie swapped the bottle into her left hand, gripping the base. She struggled to tilt it smoothly, and the wine splashed over the side of George's glass. Before she could spill any on George, the bottle was out of her hands. Gemma poured the wine herself, holding the bottle like a pro.

'Sorry,' said Annie quietly, taking her seat in the corner. 'Can't do anything right today.'

'It's all right,' Mitchell told her, concerned at the state she was in. The last thing Annie needed was her confidence being knocked.

'Wow, great,' said George as Gemma handed out the plates. And Mitchell had to admit it looked and smelled glorious. Gemma had done plantain and a separate bowl of veg. George tucked in greedily. With a quick look of apology to Annie, Mitchell tucked in, too. They were famished. And the food was amazing.

'I like hungry boys,' Gemma beamed as she took her seat with them and watched. 'This,' she said to Annie, 'is what all mealtimes should be like.'

'I'm not the one who cooks,' said Annie meekly. 'George...'

'My mum taught me to cook,' said George. 'She loved cooking for boys as well. As long as they liked their food.'

Gemma beamed, contented. The boys shovelled up their food. Between mouthfuls, George explained about the road protest. Annie wanted to know all about the radical email groups, but Gemma sat brooding until Annie noticed. She stopped mid-sentence and shut up herself. They all sat silently for a moment.

Mitchell realised Gemma didn't like Annie getting the attention. He reached out, instinctively, and squeezed Annie's hand.

'Yes,' said George, reaching for the bottle. 'Tomorrow should be good.' He'd clearly seen Annie silenced by Gemma as well, but had chosen to ignore it. Or, Mitchell realised, George was just biding his time. Good old George.

Gemma sulked in her chair. Mitchell wondered what she'd try next, and if she even knew what she was doing. He liked her, he couldn't find fault in anything she'd done, and yet being near her took work. You could feel her sapping your energy. Even as she fed you such glorious food.

When Mitchell was feeling less ravenous he sat back in his chair. Gemma immediately got up and collected the pan, doling out another helping just as generous as the first.

'Whoa,' Mitchell told her. 'I don't think I could.'

But Gemma would brook no argument. Now he felt guilty, like he'd misjudged her – she wanted nothing more than to spoil them. Mitchell again picked up his fork.

Finally the ordeal was over. George and Mitchell both sat back in their chairs, nursing swollen bellies. Mitchell reached in his pocket for a cigarette, but a look from Gemma stopped him. He folded his arms and tried to ignore the craving. After that feast, he decided, he didn't really mind at all.

Annie got up and began to clear away the things. No one said anything. Yet Mitchell saw the expression on her face. She looked terrible, as twitchy and nervous as he'd ever seen her. George noticed it too, and got up to help with the clearing.

It didn't take much to work out what was bothering Annie. Gemma sat smugly at the table, the eye of the storm of activity. And Annie begrudged her the attention.

'Gemma,' said Mitchell. 'Let's go through to the living room.' He was already on his feet, glass of wine in one hand, bottle in the other. Gemma glanced round at Annie and George, checking they were working. Then she followed Mitchell through to the sofa. Leaving Annie to the feel-good genius of George.

Mitchell and Gemma sat, side by side, a hand's width between them. Mitchell resisted the urge to move up, away from her. He sipped his wine, trying not to feel awkward.

'You'll be with us tomorrow,' said Gemma. It didn't sound like a question.

'Oh yeah,' said Mitchell. 'Wouldn't miss it. Will you be OK?'

Gemma nodded. 'Can't ignore this for ever,' she said. 'Got to do something.'

Mitchell didn't know what to say. It was like she could see into his head, and knew what he'd thought

about her, what he'd accused her of. He couldn't
think of anything to say – anything she wouldn't
already know. They sat there in awkward silence.
They heard Annie and George giggling, off in the
kitchen.

'George is a good boy,' said Gemma, echoing
Mitchell's exact thoughts.

'Yeah,' he said. 'George is great.'

'You could follow his example.'

Mitchell nodded slowly. 'I could,' he admitted.

'He doesn't think only of himself,' said Gemma.
She turned, catching Mitchell's eye then looking
away quickly.

Mitchell smiled. He had been around for a
hundred years and had seen all the tricks that there
were. Gemma wanted attention, and played games
to get it. He'd seen her play Annie, tantalising her
with approval that remained just out of reach. Keep
trying, Gemma implied, and I might just think
you worthy. The kind of thing a teenage girl did to
scramble the brain of her first boyfriend.

Mitchell was immune.

'While George was sorting the protest,' he said, 'I
found out about your son.'

She turned to face him slowly. Again he saw the
hardness in her eyes. She didn't just play mind
games; beneath the surface lurked something fierce
and determined.

'What,' she drawled, 'did you find out?'

Mitchell sat back against the sofa, sloshing more

wine into his glass. 'I think Lee was selling drugs.'

Gemma didn't even blink. 'No,' she said.

'I think so,' said Mitchell. 'A group of kids he knew all died. They'd taken something a bit like Ecstasy. Only not enough.'

He looked up, to find George and Annie in the doorway. George had a dish cloth in his hands and was casually wiping at a plate.

'Lee didn't sell drugs,' Gemma told them, no emotion in her voice.

Mitchell reached into his pocket and withdrew the folded pages. He smoothed them out, sharing with Gemma the details of Chantell Roy and Rebecca Hywel-Jones.

'These were two of them,' he said.

Gemma wouldn't even look at the pages. Her eyes were wet with tears, but she held herself perfectly poised. Still the statuesque woman, even as her world collapsed.

'They took some kind of crude amphetamine,' said Mitchell. 'They got to the hospital but by then it was too late. There was nothing anyone could do.'

Gemma shook her head. 'Was their choice to take the pills,' she said.

'Which your son sold them,' said Mitchell.

'No,' said Gemma. 'No.'

'You don't know that,' said George, coming forward.

'I reckon that's why Lee killed himself,' said Mitchell. 'He sold them the drugs, and they died.'

Gemma didn't say anything. She looked down at the pages Mitchell had passed to her.

'How could you go on after that?' said Mitchell. 'They would have been his friends.'

Still Gemma said nothing. But she moved her hand, pointing at the details on the sheets of paper. 'September,' she said.

'The fourth of September, 1999,' said Mitchell. He had her now: the dates had to prove it. 'And how soon after that did Lee die?'

Gemma looked up at him. And she smiled. Mitchell caught his breath. The look in her eyes, the delicious delight in proving him wrong...

'June,' she told him. 'Lee died at the end of June.'

Chapter
TEN

The rain spattered down, thick and heavy, filling the air with grey. Water popped and crackled in the overflowing drains, the road transformed into a dirty, litter-strewn river.

'Oh great,' said George, as they cowered in the doorway. 'We're meant to be out all day.'

Mitchell, of course, didn't say anything. He'd been sulking since the previous night, when he'd got it so wrong about Gemma's son. Lee couldn't have killed those kids – he'd been dead three months before they took the dodgy drugs.

George didn't understand why that wasn't a relief. But not even Gemma seemed happy. She'd not said a thing for the rest of the evening. He supposed that if he had a son he wouldn't like people casting aspersions. Not that he'd ever have children now.

'We can't drive to a road protest,' said Annie, stepping out into the rain. Her cardigan billowed around her, but she didn't seem to feel the cold. She didn't even lower her head against the onslaught. 'That would be weird.'

George, in his coat and hood, could hardly let her go without him. He took a step forward, splashing down into a puddle that burst up the inside of his leg. The water was cold and he hated to think how dirty. But he'd already committed himself and could only follow after Annie.

Mitchell and Gemma followed behind, studiously ignoring each other.

The weather didn't improve. They arrived on Bryn Road cold and soaked and miserable, and already most of the way through Mitchell's hip flask.

At first it looked like no one else had bothered, but as they headed down the road, a drenched gaggle of fellow travellers hailed them.

George could see little through his wet and fogged-up glasses. It took him a moment to recognise Ian with his Mohican obscured by a hood.

'Hey,' said George.

'Hey,' said Ian, and threw his arms round George for a comradely hug. George stood there, rain dripping from the end of his nose, feeling silly. He turned to Mitchell, who gave him a thumbs up.

'Come meet the others,' said Ian, letting George go. 'I've told them all about you.'

They were an assorted bunch, George had to admit. An Indian woman with her head in a scarf under the hood of her coat. A huge man called Mike who usually manned a recording desk and had, he said, mixed albums George felt he should have heard of. He thought he had met Ian's boyfriend Danny before, and he knew Kaz's girlfriend Gail, plus some of the other nurses who'd been in the meeting the day before. They all had rucksacks and bags of equipment. George felt decidedly under-prepared.

He and Mitchell shook hands with the group in turn, thanking them for coming. Annie and Gemma stood just apart from everyone else, invisible even to the rain. Gemma wore her smart purple coat and hat over her floral dress and lacquered hair. She at least looked dressed up to face a day in the rain. Annie only had on her leggings, white T-shirt and cardie.

Mitchell went over to cajole them into joining in, but no one else seemed able to see them, and his fellow protesters watching him bemusedly.

'He's got one of those mobile phones with an earpiece,' George explained to them. 'Makes him look like he's talking to the air. Not that there's anything wrong with talking to the air. He could be doing that as well, and that would be fine. But, as I say, he's got one of those mobile phones with an earpiece.'

'It's all right,' one of the nurses told him. 'We don't

need to drag any more people down here. This will be enough.'

'OK!' said Ian loudly, once all the introductions had been made. All eyes were on him. The rain clattered down on their hoods and coats.

'We're going to head down the road,' announced Ian, 'and find places that look like we could defend them. They might try to stop us. Some of you know what that's like.' A few of the protesters murmured their assent. George glanced round. None of them looked like hardened subversives. They looked less resolved than just bored and wanting to get on with it.

'We've got supplies,' said Ian. 'Bottles of water, in case they use tear gas. Someone goes down with that, you squirt it in their eyes. Anything else, well a good few of us are first-aiders. First-aiders raise your hands.'

About a third of the group put their hands up, Mitchell included. George looked to Mitchell. What had they got themselves involved in? They surely didn't expect a fight. Mitchell grinned back at him. He'd always liked a fight.

'We've got a single goal,' Ian continued. 'We want people to know that enough is enough. We can't go on building roads over everything.'

No one took up the cry, they just stood there, in the rain.

Ian grinned at them. 'Well,' he said. 'Best get going.'

They set off, moving slowly in the wind and the rain. George didn't feel very enthusiastic and he'd been the one behind this protest. He hated to think how anyone else felt. He glanced round at them, and made eye contact with Gail. To his horror she made her way over to join him. He'd always found her difficult, and he knew she hated Mitchell.

'George,' she said.

'Gail,' he said. She was wearing a low-cut V-neck that exposed a lot of ample cleavage and the lower edge of her bra. George tried not to look, but he couldn't help it. 'Didn't think this would be your thing.'

'The planet needs us to play our part,' she told him, and didn't seem to be joking.

George nodded. 'Yeah,' he said.

'I didn't know you were an activist, too,' she said. George wasn't sure what to say to that, but Gail didn't let him respond anyway. 'It's good to see Mitchell is here. Kaz wants me and him to make things up.'

George glanced over at Mitchell, walking between Gemma and Annie. He looked, thought George, like he was keeping them apart.

'Yeah?' said George. 'Mitchell's OK.'

'I didn't think so at first,' said Gail. 'It's just... Well, not everyone would turn up to something like this. I'm only here because Kaz told me I had to come. She's covering my shift so I can do this. Says it's important for our children.'

George shrugged. 'I didn't know you had any children.'

Gail looked up at him, mouth hanging open and eyes wide. 'I don't,' she said.

'Sorry,' said George. 'I just meant…' The awful thought struck him. 'Kaz was at the meeting yesterday. So you're… trying.'

Gail nodded, her expression serious. 'It's very trying,' she said.

George gulped. 'I…' he said. 'Look, forget I said anything.' He wanted to show he understood. 'It's not easy, is it?'

'No,' she agreed. 'No one understands.'

'If there was something I could do,' said George.

'It just takes such a long time to get pregnant,' Gail told him. 'I mean, if there are complications and you don't have a male partner. Everything assumes you're in a normal hetero relationship.'

'Define "normal",' said George.

Gail laughed. She linked her arm in his, hugging him as they walked. Her head nestled against his upper arm. He didn't mind. She was warm against him, and seemed to like him, too. He never understood why some people just attached themselves to him, but he rather liked that they did.

'And then it gets so expensive,' Gail went on. 'Three and a half thousand pounds for the treatment, another thousand for the drugs, and that's each time you have to do it.'

George stopped listening as she explained the problems of family and friends who didn't understand the process or what the hormones did to your head, or who always asked questions so that every conversation felt like an exam. Instead, George took in the street they were trying to protect.

The houses were late Victorian and early twentieth century. They'd been built with fireplaces in every room, the network of chimneys visible on the exterior side walls, like the branches of an upturned tree. A few had double glazing, but most still had wooden sash windows. This had once been a smart, respectable street, but time and the city were moving on. The street had fallen into disrepair; those with the get-go to look after their homes had all long since moved away.

He wondered which of the buildings were lived in now. There were no cars parked outside, and the small oblongs of front garden had long been untended. He glanced up and down, looking for lights on in the rain. No, there didn't seem any sign of life.

Ten years ago, squatters had lived here. It made George smile to think of them – the lowest in the social order, a sure sign of the end of the road. And the houses, a century old and yet built to last, taking them in. That, he thought, was real craftsmanship.

He realised Gail was still going on, now about some bloke who behaved like a pig. He seemed to be making Kaz and her girlfriend's life a nightmare.

'Then don't see him any more,' advised George.

'Hah!' said Gail. 'He's my brother. That's why we chose him in the first place. But now I think it's too close, too weird.' She clung on to George's arm, so tight she might have bruised him. 'But like Kaz says, who else would we go to?'

George sighed. He knew what Gail wanted him to do. She needed someone to fight her corner. He liked Gail, he realised. And he didn't like the idea of her being ganged up on, and over something so important.

'All right,' he said. 'I could intercede.'

She let go of his arm and stared up at him. 'Kaz *said* she thought you'd help us.'

George smiled at her. 'If you think it would make things easier,' he said.

Gail continued to stare up at him. She had beautiful hazel eyes and skin the colour of milky coffee. 'You and Mitchell…' she said.

George was wounded by that. 'He doesn't need to hold my hand,' he said. 'I can handle myself.'

A smile twitched Gail's face. She took George's arm again, this time hugging him close. 'You're a nice man,' she said. 'There aren't many of those around.'

'I know,' sighed George, hugging her back. Women often said that: he was always a friend to them, rarely anything more. But that was OK. After Nina and everything, that's all he wanted for the moment.

He felt good, a knight in armour helping two damsels in distress.

He glanced round at the other protesters. No one else seemed to be talking. Ian, up front, looked sullen because they'd not found the right kind of house yet nor anyone to fight. Everyone else looked wet and miserable, regretting that they'd turned up.

George wondered what he and Gail must look like to them, arms round one another, as if having a whale of a time. And what had he just agreed to?

'I should make things up with Mitchell,' said Gail. 'Or this is all going to be awkward.'

'Mitchell?' asked George.

What had Mitchell got to do with it?

The thought struck him like a thunderbolt. Gail thought he was Mitchell's boyfriend. He thought through his conversation with Kaz yesterday, when he'd wandered into the meeting. Oh God, he thought, Kaz had seen him with Ian and put two and two together. All gays together, like on one of those late-night advertisements for phone lines. Was that what everyone thought?

With dread realisation, he played over again the events of the previous few days, the odd conversations he'd had with Mossy, and with Sarah on reception. Hadn't they seen him with Nina? Was that why they thought she'd run off?

And now, somehow, Gail the lesbian, hugging him tight, thought he could sort things out with her brother. Like he was some kind of tough guy.

The last thing he needed was another fight.

He had to make sure he didn't say anything else. George continued walking, Gail under his arm, letting the rain prickle against his face. Say nothing, he thought, and things couldn't get worse or weirder.

They could see the end of the road ahead of them, the last few, unoccupied houses on each side. There were signs and traffic cones warning of the building work, but no other signs of life. Mitchell listened for diggers and bulldozers, or the heartbeats of the demolition men. He could hear nothing but the rain. The protest had been a waste of time. He wondered how long it would take Ian and the others to realise that.

Ian, though, had found his element. Three of the houses were boarded up, chipboard panels over the front doors and windows. These were the buildings they could get into – they just needed to pick out the nails.

Ian began to unpack his rucksack, piling the contents in the rain-slick road. A bag of fun-size Mars bars, a travel towel and wash bag, a water bottle and a spare pair of shoes. Then he produced a hammer with a y-shaped back end, and set to the chipboard panels with a vengeance.

Another protester had also come with tools, and soon they were working on houses on opposite sides of the street. The other protesters cheered and chatted among themselves, enthused by the activity and promise of getting out of the rain.

Mitchell lagged behind the others, watching Gemma and Annie. They didn't say anything to one another, but Mitchell recognised the signs. Annie was in Gemma's thrall.

He didn't like Gemma, he had decided. There was something about her. Something that needled at him.

He couldn't say anything to Annie or George, though. They'd say he was just in a mood because Gemma had proven him wrong. His conspiracy theory about her son had turned out to be so much hot air. The look in her eyes when he'd confronted her! She'd known he'd got it completely wrong.

Because she knew exactly why her son killed himself.

The idea gnawed at his insides. That had to be it; that had to be the cause of the hardness in her eyes. And that was why she'd not been more excited by the stuff Annie had found in the library. The road and its importance weren't a surprise to her. She already knew why she'd come back through the door.

How could he confront her? How could he prove what she knew? Something Annie and George couldn't doubt.

All the time Mitchell watched Gemma as the protesters wrenched the chipboard panels from the houses. A couple of women seemed bored with the waiting, and broke the window of one the houses that hadn't been boarded up. At first the protesters seemed scared by this development. They all glanced round at each other, even Ian, and Mitchell could see them ready to flee. But no one stopped them, no one cried out, and the two women were emboldened. One gave the other a leg up, and soon she was through the broken glass and into the house. A moment later the front door opened, and she welcomed the protesters in to a delighted cheer.

But Mitchell stood where he was in the rain, puzzling over Gemma. Was that what she'd done to her son, as well? Made him feel guilty and stupid whatever the care that he showed her?

Gemma was like some kind of spider, pulling the strings of the web and drawing them all in. She presented this meek and vulnerable front, but she was more powerful than any of them. Look at what George had laid on for her, all these people out in the rain.

Gemma glanced back at him and caught his eye. Again he saw the hardness inside her, the defiant strength. And she must have seen him staring determinedly back.

He smiled at her, baring his teeth, an animal challenge. There was a tang in the air, the pungent, industrial stink that clung round Gemma.

It came from the house with the broken window, too. Mitchell noticed the number on the door.

Number 8, Bryn Road. The house where Lee had died.

With a start, he looked back at Gemma.

Her eyes were wide, as if the stink choked her. Mitchell stepped forward, but Gemma threw up her hands, as if to fight him off. Soundless, strangled, eyes bulging in their sockets, she collapsed onto the rain-drenched pavement.

Annie stood there, mute with horror.

The protesters couldn't see her as they shoved past. Yet they could all see Gemma, prone on the pavement, her right arm in a puddle. Annie felt suddenly exposed, though as they shoved past her she knew that she remained invisible. For a moment she wanted to be seen, to have some share of the attention.

But the look on Gemma's face stilled her. Her dark eyes bulged, her mouth twisted in an awful snarl of terror.

Mitchell ran forward, taking charge.

'Don't touch her,' he said. His voice had such anger and authority the protesters did as they were told. They shrank back, letting him get in to crouch by Gemma's body.

George joined Annie, a pretty black girl, with huge tits, clinging round his waist. Annie didn't like the look of her much, and flared her nostrils at George. George rolled his eyes – he didn't like the girl either, Annie was sure. She smiled; they couldn't acknowledge each other now, not without drawing attention. They could discuss it later over a nice cup of tea.

Mitchell was helping Gemma to sit up. Annie felt a chill run through her. What had Gemma seen, or sensed? Annie glanced back up and down the road, but could see nothing out of the ordinary. And yet she could feel the emptiness of the buildings, the memories evaporating from them. If she put her hand out towards one of the houses she might grasp a moment that happened inside. A child's first birthday, a married woman having an affair, a boy with a rope round his neck. Gemma's son!

She cried out, feeling the memory clutch around her.

'No!'

Then she was back in the street, standing under the rain that never touched her, George just by her side. He stared down at Gemma and the crowd of protesters around her. Annie reached out to touch his arm, shaken that he'd not heard her cry out.

She touched bare flesh and recoiled. Annie had stroked her fingers against the black girl's hands. The girl moved and, for a moment, Annie thought the girl had seen her. But no, she nuzzled against George again, like some sickly lamb.

'Don't fuss,' Annie heard Gemma say.

'I think it's the rain,' Mitchell announced to the crowd. 'Just got a bit cold, lost her balance.'

'There's something in the house,' said the woman

who'd climbed through the window. 'I could feel its aura.'

Some of the protesters backed quickly away from number 8. The front door stood open, like a wound. Nothing stirred within.

Annie didn't want to venture any further. She knew what angry ghosts could do. Instead, she focused on Gemma, coming to her senses.

'She doesn't look very wet,' said the man with the earrings in his lip. Annie thought he was George's friend, Ian.

'She doesn't,' Mitchell agreed. 'So we just have to be careful.'

'I'm fine,' Gemma told them. If no one had seen her on the protest before she'd had her fall, they didn't say anything. The statuesque black woman in her smart coat and hat didn't look like one of them, thought Annie. But they were probably grateful for anyone who came along.

'Let me help you,' said Mitchell, getting Gemma to her feet. She stood there, weak and confused, surrounded by the protesters. And Annie felt a sudden flash of anger at being the only one no one could see.

'Um,' said George. 'Someone's coming.'

They all turned. A dark green car crawled slowly towards them, its fog lights cutting through the rain. Gemma didn't know her cars but it looked old and angular, maybe from the 1980s. The engine growled much louder than a modern car.

The protesters fanned out around the car, enveloping it. The car drew to a halt.

With all eyes on the new arrival, Annie made her way over to Gemma. 'Are you all right?' she asked.

'I'm fine,' Gemma insisted. 'I don't like all this fuss.'

Annie recoiled. She felt stupid for envying Gemma the attention. And she could see the horror still there in Gemma's eyes. 'I felt it, too,' she said.

Gemma glared at her. But then her expression softened. Annie knew what she must be feeling, the relief that someone else understood.

'His house,' said Gemma, nodding across the road to number 8.

Annie stared at the impassive front of the building. It didn't look much, just an ordinary terrace in dark red bricks. But the open door and the darkness beyond were terrifying to behold. She felt the ground trembling underneath her, had to reach out to Gemma to steady herself.

'I can't go in there,' said Gemma.

'No,' said Annie. 'There's something in there. Something other than your son.'

Gemma nodded. 'My son,' she said, 'isn't in there. But something is. Something… *bad.*'

And Annie knew she was right. 'Come on,' she said, taking Gemma's arm, leading her away from the place where her son died, and over to the living people, crowding round the car.

*

Mitchell and Ian stood by the driver's side window as it slowly wound down. Gavin Foot poked his head out of the old Ford Fiesta and gave them a winning smile.

'Mitchell!' he said. 'Not all over, is it?'

'This is Gavin,' Mitchell explained to Ian. 'Works for the *Daily Press*. Thought he could spread the word about what we're doing.'

Ian scowled down at Gavin. 'You came in a car,' he said.

Gavin grinned. 'Thought you might have something to say about that.'

Mitchell backed away as Gavin scrambled out into the rain, waving around a handheld recording device with two tiny mikes on the end. Ian made a number of grand pronouncements about everything they were achieving, which Gavin didn't interrupt. He could clearly see there were no police or workmen around, and only a dozen protesters. But rather than put that to Ian immediately, he'd let Ian hang himself first.

'Don't you want to say something?' asked George, all touchy feely with Gail. She looked up at Mitchell and grinned, then let go of George.

'Nah,' said Mitchell. 'Not really one for the limelight.'

'But you could have your picture in the paper,' grinned George. Mitchell turned back to find Gavin getting the protesters to pose for his camera. Without much encouragement, the protesters struck all the clichés. At best, thought Mitchell, they'd look bedraggled and well-meaning.

But George wasn't just teasing. They both knew that Mitchell wouldn't show up in any photos, that he had to keep back from the crowd. Mitchell couldn't let Gavin stumble upon his secret – for Gavin's sake as well as his own.

'You talk to him if you like,' he told George.

'Me?' said George.

'Yeah,' Mitchell teased. 'You've got a gift for putting things simply, so there's no misunderstanding.'

'Have I?' said George, delighted. Before Mitchell could stop him, George had waded into the throng around Gavin. 'I'm George,' he said. 'I'm the one who called you this morning.'

Gavin blinked up at George, struck by his size and easy manner. For a moment, Gavin stood frozen, then he thrust out his hand. 'George,' he said. 'Sure. Pleased to meet you. Why don't you tell me everything?'

Mitchell laughed as George started to explain. He could see Gavin's smile becoming more and more fixed behind his recording device, the look of a man who knows he's got his work cut out for him in the transcription. George had an unearthly skill in mangling the sense out of a sentence.

Mitchell turned to Annie and Gemma, standing apart on the pavement away from everyone else. The breeze flapped Annie's cardigan, but otherwise the weather didn't touch them. They looked haggard.

Gemma seemed to have faded away again so that none of the living could see her. Mitchell wondered if she was even aware of it, or of where she was. Both ghosts stared at the gang of protesters and the journalist, but it was like they looked right through them.

Had he misjudged Gemma? The fall has been genuine. When he'd run over to her, prone on the pavement, he'd seen the terror in her eyes. Even he could feel the dark presence inside the nearby house. Something had reached out and grabbed her, something she wasn't ready to face. He'd thought that her lack of reaction to all they'd found out was a sign she didn't care. But how else could you feel about losing a son?

He would have gone over to her, but Gail stopped him.

'Um,' she said.

He smiled. 'You and George looked cosy,' he said.

'No,' she said. 'Yes,' she said. 'We've come to an agreement.'

'That's George,' he told her. He couldn't help notice the way Gail glanced over his shoulder at George. Or the deep bass of her heart, thumping under her breast. Despite the rain and cold, her whole body glowed with warmth. Mitchell smiled. 'You seem to like him.'

'Yeah,' she said. 'I think so. He's a good man.'

'So there's no problem,' said Mitchell. 'Is there?'

Gail nodded. 'Me and Kaz, we're looking for a good man to help us out,' she said.

Mitchell grinned. Trust George to stumble his way into a threesome. 'George is in a funny place right now. Maybe he could do with some female company.'

Gail stared at him. 'You don't mind…?'

Oh yeah, thought Mitchell. He and George were meant to be a couple. 'I want George to be happy,' he said, and tried to look noble about it, too. He seemed to spend his whole time helping poor George to get laid.

Gail nodded. 'I don't know,' she said. 'It would make some things easier. But I'll have to talk to Kaz.' But Mitchell could read the signals; it was just a matter of time. George owed him one.

'It'll be fine,' he said. 'George will look after you.'

Gail smiled up at him. 'I misjudged you,' she said. 'I apologise.'

'Hey,' said Mitchell. 'We're almost family now.'

'Mitchell!' George squeaked from over by the car. Honestly, Mitchell couldn't leave him for five minutes.

He turned, to see George waving frantically. Mitchell began to say, 'What?' as Gail threw her arms tight around him. Something exploded in his face.

Green and purple dots danced before his eyes. He tried to swipe them away with one hand as the world and the rain came back into focus. Gail let him go, laughing. But Mitchell didn't even see her.

He could only see Gavin, turning away from them, raising his camera to snap someone else.

Gavin had taken his picture.

Chapter
ELEVEN

George and Mitchell nodded at each other. They both knew what had to be their priority now: they had to get hold of Gavin's camera and erase the picture he'd taken. The picture Mitchell would not appear in. Mitchell's doubts about Gemma could wait.

Gavin had the camera on a strap round his neck, and there was no way to reach it without drawing undue attention. George tried to get close, hands out, fingers twitching ready. Mitchell hurried over, taking George's arm.

'We need to be subtle,' he said.

'Subtle,' said George. 'I can do subtle.'

'George,' Mitchell told him. 'Maybe just leave this to me.'

They kept out of Gavin's way as he continued to

snap pictures of the protesters, making themselves at home in the houses they'd got into. Number 8 they left alone, but number 9 opposite and number 6 next door would be where they'd make their stand.

Those who were staying went into the houses. Those who were not hung around outside. But apart from Gavin there was no one around to protest *to*. There didn't seem to be any point hanging around in the rain. Gavin had spoken to all those who wanted to speak to him and had, he told them, more than enough for an initial story. He'd come back later, and see if they'd been noticed.

'I should go,' said Gail. She started to walk away, then hurried back, reaching up on tiptoe to kiss George on the cheek. 'I'll see you,' she said, 'when I've spoken to Kaz.' She ran off.

George stroked the cold, numb skin she had kissed, staring after her.

'Will you just *stop*,' Mitchell chided, a cheesy grin on his face. 'You've worked your way through all the straight ones, now you're converting the lesbians.'

George rolled his eyes.

'Care to share any pointers?' asked Gavin.

'You've either got it,' grinned George, 'or you haven't.'

He looked across the road to where Annie and Gemma stood on the far pavement. Gemma stared forlornly at the front of number 8, where her son had died. Annie had her arms crossed, like she could finally feel the cold. When she saw George looking, she gestured with one thumb over her shoulder and mouthed the single word, 'Home'.

She reached out her hand to Gemma's shoulder. George must have blinked, and then the women were gone. He sighed at the thought of them, back in the house they wouldn't know was warm, making tea they couldn't drink.

'Where you guys heading?' said Gavin. 'I could drop you home.'

'Great,' said Mitchell.

'Er, yeah, OK,' said George. 'That would save us getting...' He stopped, looking down at himself. 'Well. We're already soaked.'

They made their way back to Gavin's green Ford Fiesta, the old, boxy shape they'd stopped making sometime in the mid 1990s. George had had a mate who drove a purple one, back when they were 17.

'So,' said Mitchell as Gavin struggled to get the driver's seat to tip forward so one of them could scramble into the back. 'We're going to have our pictures in the paper.'

'I can't promise,' said Gavin, through gritted teeth. 'But I'll try.'

'And what sort of camera have you got there?' asked Mitchell. 'One of these new high-resolution digital things?'

George could see him already reaching forward to take the camera hanging round Gavin's neck. Mitchell would just scroll through the pictures, then accidentally delete the one he didn't appear in.

'No, 'fraid not,' said Gavin, standing back up. 'Old-fashioned film in this. Can't beat the depth of field, and you don't get that grainy effect.'

'Wow,' said Mitchell, not put off for a second. 'Haven't seen one of those in ages. Can I have a look?'

Gavin hesitated, but then lifted the strap from round the back of his neck and handed the camera to Mitchell. Mitchell admired the thing, squinting through the viewfinder and whirling round to ready different shots of the street. He grinned like a child with a new toy, trying the different settings. The flash clicked out of its housing. The lens whirred forward as he pointed the thing right at George.

'Nice bit of kit,' said George, taking the camera and handing it back towards Gavin. And then it was tumbling out of his hand.

'Whoa,' said Mitchell, stepping forward to grab the camera, at the same time shouldering into Gavin, knocking him back out of reach.

The camera thumped the tarmac hard, water splashing up around it. It bounced and came down hard again, turning over on its side. But it didn't break.

George, Mitchell and Gavin all stared at it, sat on its side in a puddle.

'Christ,' said Mitchell.

'Yeah,' said George.

'Takes more than that to damage this thing,' said Gavin. 'I dropped it out of a train window, once.

Can hardly tell it's scratched.'

He scooted forward to collect the camera, glancing over it to make sure it still worked.

'But your pictures will be OK?' asked Mitchell.

'Oh yeah,' Gavin told him, standing back so Mitchell could climb into the back seat of the car.

Mitchell glanced back at George as he climbed into the car. 'I'm really sorry, anyway' he said as he hauled his legs round so that he could sit diagonally across the back seat. 'Maybe we can take you for a pint.'

George climbed into the front passenger seat. Old paperbacks and magazines crowded around his feet. It looked as if Gavin used his car for stake-outs. Or just wasn't very tidy.

'Yeah,' said Gavin, getting in behind the wheel. 'I'd like that. Here.' He twisted round to hand Mitchell the camera. 'You look after this.'

'Oh, I will,' said Mitchell. 'I promise.'

They found themselves back in the living room. Gemma shrugged her shoulder free of Annie's hand and without a word sat down on the leather sofa. As if she'd never been away she started again on the Inspector Morse jigsaw.

Annie stared at her. All the tension and horror gone from the woman's face. She sat poised and serene, still in her coat and hat.

Annie wanted to yell at her. What had they just witnessed? What had reached out of the house at number 8, and given Gemma such a shock? Now they were so far back, and back in Annie's house, surely they had to talk.

But Gemma sat there, studiously working on her jigsaw.

'There was something in that house,' said Annie.

'There was,' Gemma told her, not even deigning to look up.

'Something terrible,' said Annie.

Gemma sighed. 'Yes,' she said. 'I don't ever want to go back there.'

'But there's something behind all this!'

Gemma looked up at her, and Annie almost gasped at the cruel sneer on her face.

'I'm sorry,' she said quickly. 'I just want to help.'

Gemma shook her head slowly, all the time her eyes fixed on Annie. 'I know,' she said. 'But what can you do that will help me?'

Annie didn't have an answer. Gemma gazed up at her, waiting for a response. Then she sighed and returned to her jigsaw.

Annie felt light-headed. She tottered to the wall, and slid down it to the floor. Sat on the ground, hugging her knees, she felt a little better. Perhaps the cold and rain had hit her. Perhaps whatever she'd sensed in number 8 had hit her harder than she thought. But Annie felt spent, her light exhausted.

And for the first time since she'd died, she slept.

Gavin parked on their road, just a bit up from the

house and in front of the wall on which was painted *Keep clear, 24hr access*. They had a choice of pubs – indeed, as George stepped out of the car he was under an awning for one of them. The board above his head showed an old-fashioned ship with Bristol's famous suspension bridge behind it.

But Mitchell had a thing for the Shakespeare, further down the road, so that's where they took Gavin. Mitchell seemed jubilant. He handed Gavin's camera to George and said he wanted to pose for pictures. George indulged him, knowing Mitchell must have swiped the film.

They got into the pub. Their favourite table, with the deep, comfy chairs, was taken, so they perched at the bar drinking lager.

'Cheers,' said Mitchell. 'And sorry. If anything happened to that camera…'

'No problem,' said Gavin. 'No damage done. Really.' He turned to George, involving him. 'So how's things at work?'

'OK,' said George, aware he was talking to a journalist. Saying anything out of turn might well lose him his job.

'Gavin's OK,' said Mitchell. 'You can talk to him.'

George nodded but didn't have anything else to say.

'I've talked to other people, too,' said Gavin. 'They think the missing paperwork is something else. It's a trail they want me to find. I expose stuff going on and the new administrator gets carte blanche. He can change what he likes, chuck anyone out. What do you think of that?'

Mitchell drank his lager. 'Maybe,' he said.

'You don't believe it,' said Gavin.

'I didn't say that,' Mitchell told him. 'But there's still something about those kids from 1999.'

'You've found out something else,' said Gavin, sitting forward eagerly.

'No,' Mitchell admitted. 'But I'm looking.'

'I've got evidence,' Gavin told them. 'Records have been altered or destroyed. It's difficult to judge how far it goes back or how widespread it is. There are dead ends wherever you look. Someone's got to be doing this on purpose.'

'I'm looking,' said Mitchell.

Gavin nodded. 'I know. I appreciate it. But I'm on a deadline. My editor needs a story by tomorrow night.'

They sat there, nursing their beers. Then a thought struck George.

'But you've got the road protest,' he said.

Gavin nodded. 'Yes,' he said, though he didn't sound convinced.

'You don't think your editor will be interested?' asked Mitchell.

'It's just not a story we can sell. All the arguments have been heard before. And our readers worry about their mortgages. They won't side with the squatters, whatever they're trying to achieve.'

'It's a good story,' said George.

'I know,' said Gavin. 'I can probably get a couple of columns, if the pictures come out all right.'

George and Mitchell exchanged glances, but they both knew that their hands were tied.

They saw Gavin into his car and waved him off, Mitchell clutching the roll of film in his hand. Once the green Ford Fiesta had turned the corner, George turned to Mitchell.

'You're in the clear,' he said. 'But at what cost?'

Mitchell still stared after Gavin's car. 'He needs a story by tomorrow night,' he said. 'Come on, this isn't over.'

They headed up the street to their door. Mitchell stopped, the key almost up to the lock. He looked back at George.

'Gemma collapsed,' he said. 'Because of whatever's in that house.'

'I know,' sighed George. 'But if she's going to tell us, we have to be subtle.'

Mitchell looked affronted. 'I can be subtle,' he said.

'You weren't last night when you confronted her,' said George.

Mitchell considered this. 'Then tonight will be different.'

Annie woke with a start as they came in. Surprised and muzzy, she got to her feet and ran to greet them.

'I was asleep!' she told them. But the boys didn't seem to hear.

They were drenched and miserable, but Annie could also tell that they'd stopped off at the pub on their way home. They dripped on the black and white tiles, shrugging off their sodden coats.

'Did you get the picture?' she asked Mitchell. He handed her the roll of film. Annie grinned at him, wide-eyed. 'How?'

'I can be very persuasive,' said Mitchell. He didn't smile. In fact, he seemed to be holding back his fury.

'What?' said Annie.

'Where is she?' said Mitchell. Annie looked round into the living room. Gemma wasn't on the sofa. They looked into the kitchen, but there was no Gemma there either.

They trooped upstairs, George and Mitchell leaving wet footprints on the carpet. Annie sighed; she'd have to vacuum later. They made their way down the landing to Annie's room, to find Gemma sitting in the armchair. She still wore her coat and hat, her hands folded in her lap. Annie thought she might have been praying, or just staring into space.

'Gemma,' said Mitchell.

She gradually raised her head – and it seemed to Annie as if she couldn't quite see them. Gemma had been severely shaken by the attack out on the road. She'd not wanted to talk about it, or to have Annie talk to her. She'd just slunk off up here, brooding alone with her thoughts.

'The journalist,' said Mitchell. 'He's going to print the story tomorrow. About the kids who took the drugs.'

Gemma nodded slowly.

'They knew your son, didn't they?' said Mitchell.

Gemma stared up at him. 'He didn't sell them drugs,' she said. 'He didn't have anything to do with it. Your friend can print what he likes.'

Mitchell folded his arms. 'But you know something, don't you? You've always known what really happened. That's why none of this is a surprise. We find things out about how your son died, and you just sit here doing jigsaws.'

Gemma stared back at him, and Annie saw the change in her eyes. The hardness, the defiance. She seemed so tough and powerful when Annie just felt lousy.

Gemma, though, said nothing.

'I felt it,' said Annie. 'When we passed the house on Bryn Road.'

'Don't,' Gemma told her.

'I could feel the memories leaking out,' Annie told George and Mitchell. 'The pain, still raw after all this time. It reached out for us. Like it was hungry.'

'You don't know what you're talking about,' snapped Gemma.

Annie flinched, falling back.

George caught her in his arms. 'What's happening?' he said. 'What's wrong?'

'I was asleep,' Annie beamed up at him. She liked being in George's arms. He always made her feel safe.

'What's wrong with Annie?' said George.

'She's fading,' said Mitchell. 'Something's sapping her strength.' Annie watched him turn on Gemma. 'Isn't it?'

Annie felt something change in the air. As Gemma looked up at Mitchell, Annie felt a warmth around her.

'I don't know,' said Gemma, miserably. 'I don't know how any of this works.'

'You must know,' said Mitchell. 'It's all about you.'

'Don't shout,' murmured Gemma, though Mitchell hadn't been shouting. 'It hurts me when you shout.'

Annie shrugged off George's arm. She felt like the fug had lifted, like she could breathe again. And she couldn't stand Gemma sat low in the chair, Mitchell standing over her.

'Leave her alone,' she told him.

Mitchell turned in surprise. 'Annie,' he said. 'You're not—'

'I'm fine,' Annie told him, pushing past to reach Gemma.

Gemma looked up at her. 'I don't know what's happening,' she said.

'I know,' said Annie. 'And there's only one way we can find out.'

Gemma looked up at her, and it took a moment for her to understand. Fear filled her eyes. 'No.'

Annie reached out, taking Gemma's hand. 'It's all right,' she said. 'I stopped vampires. I beat Owen. I'm not going to let anything happen to you.'

'Please,' said Gemma, but she had no fight.

Annie glanced back at George and Mitchell. 'We can't ignore it for ever,' she told them.

'Don't—' Mitchell cried out.

But Annie squeezed Gemma's hand in hers and –

– they were somewhere else.

The room was dark and stank of something. Annie struggled to see in the gloom. A long, oblong living room, a kitchen through a door at the back, a flight of stairs ahead of the front door, standing open on to the dark street. There was no furniture and only patches of carpet, which meant the house sounded eerie, Annie's breath echoing all around.

'No!' said Gemma, eyes wide with horror as she realised where they were. Number 8, Bryn Road, had not been lived in for years.

Gemma tried to shake Annie off, but Annie held on to her arm. She couldn't let Gemma escape. They had to face whatever was here.

They turned at the sound behind them. The room stood abandoned and still.

'We're here,' Annie told the empty room, her voice wavering with her own fear. 'You can come out now.'

Nothing.

And then there came a glimpse of pallid, silver light.

'No!' mouthed Gemma in horror as the ghosts came forward.

Chapter
TWELVE

Annie wanted to reach out to them, comfort them. The three ghosts shimmered in the air, their skin and clothes translucent like smoked glass. They were so young, she thought, even younger than her. Eighteen-year-olds, in the T-shirts and jeans and those trousers that hung low off their hips so you could see their pants.

Fashion hasn't changed that much in the last ten years, thought Annie. *These kids could have died just yesterday.*

She could see through them, see the faded, peeling wallpaper of the wall behind them. The ghosts stared blankly, their mouths hanging open, their arms outstretched. But they had long forgotten how to make themselves heard.

'I'm Annie,' she told them kindly. She didn't feel

afraid. Bizarrely, she hadn't felt so strong in ages. 'I'm like you. I died.'

The ghosts stared back at her impassively. She didn't know if they could understand.

Beside her, Gemma quivered with fear. The woman seemed paralysed, rooted to the spot. She too seemed unable to speak.

'It's all right,' Annie told the ghosts. 'We want to help. There must be something, a reason you're all here. Once we know, we can send you on your way.'

The ghosts shimmered in front of them. One of them, a boy of Chinese descent, nodded his head.

'OK,' said Annie. She prodded Gemma. 'This is Gemma. Do you know who she is?'

The ghosts didn't turn their heads or acknowledge Gemma's presence. Yet the Chinese boy slowly shook his head.

'No,' said Gemma in an agonised whisper. 'I was only his mum.' A tear ran down her cheek. Annie felt awful. She knew how hard it had been for her when Mitchell and George had tried to make her face how she'd died and why she'd not moved on. But they had to face whatever had brought Gemma back and kept these poor spirits trapped in this drab old house.

'Her son used to live here,' Annie went on. 'A boy called Lee.' The ghosts didn't react to the name, so Annie had to ask. 'Did you know him?'

Slowly, the Chinese boy nodded his head.

His eyes still stared blankly. Annie felt a rush of excitement and fear course through her. They were on to something.

'He died in this house,' said Annie. The Chinese boy nodded his head.

'It was you,' said Gemma. 'You sent me these photographs.'

Annie turned, surprised. Gemma's whole body shook as she pointed at the teenage ghosts. 'They broke him down. Bullied him. The people he shared this house with. His friends.' She took a deep breath, standing up straight, more her old, defiant self. 'Isn't that right?'

To Annie's horror, the Chinese boy nodded. He raised his head towards the stairs and the darkness they led up to. His jaw twitched, struggling to remember the method of speaking after all the long years.

'Uh,' he said.

'What is it?' Annie asked him.

He struggled again and the word came. 'Rope.'

From the banister on the landing hung a silver cord of rope. It shimmered, made of the same ghostly material as the translucent teens. Annie shuddered at the sight of it, Gemma let out a low gasp. These ghosts, these stupid, selfish kids. They were haunted themselves by the terrible thing they had done.

Annie nodded. 'You're being punished,' she said. 'That's why you're here.'

The Chinese boy nodded. His eyes were pitiful black holes, no spark behind them. The teenagers were barely ghosts at all, they'd just decayed into the air. Annie couldn't think of a worse fate, everything you were just unravelling piece by piece.

'But you died,' she said. 'You took those pills and you died.'

The Chinese boy stared back at her with those dark and awful sockets. He said nothing.

'It must have been an accident,' said Gemma. Annie turned to her. Gemma kept staring at the shimmering teens, her expression stern. She seemed stronger, just at hearing the ghosts admit it had been their fault. Annie felt a swell of pride for daring to bring her here.

'It was fate,' she said.

The Chinese boy nodded. 'We,' he said, a strangled whisper. 'We deserved it.'

The first they knew that the girls were coming back was the tang in the air, the itchy, industrial aroma that preceded Gemma. George and Mitchell hurried back up to Annie's room, to find Gemma, shaken, collapsed into the armchair, pulling off her hat and coat. Tears ran in tracks down her cheeks and her bottom lip trembled. But when George and Mitchell tried to approach, she waved them away crossly.

Annie staggered at the exertion, but waved off their attempts to help them. She led the boys out onto the landing and told them what she had seen. Mitchell could give the Chinese boy a name. 'Thomas Ho,' he said. 'He and the others got as far as A&E. He died that night, haemorrhage and liver failure.'

'And he's been in that house ever since?' said George. 'Poor bloke.'

'They killed Gemma's son,' Annie reminded him. 'They led him to it.'

'Even so,' said George. 'It's been ten years. Isn't that enough?'

'Where did they get the drugs?' asked Mitchell.

'A dealer,' said George. 'Sometimes they're dodgy.'

'And you are such the expert,' said Mitchell.

'No,' said George. 'But I've read the pamphlets up in A&E. They can tell you a lot, about drugs and VD and fireworks.'

'After it's too late,' said Mitchell. 'And you're in A&E.'

'Well,' said George. 'How do you explain it, then?'

'It's fate,' said Annie. 'They killed Lee so they had to be punished.'

'It doesn't work like that,' said Mitchell. 'Life is just unfair.'

'So, go on then,' said George. 'Amaze us.'

Mitchell scowled. 'I don't know,' he said. 'It's not just the pills. Someone changed the hospital records. Tried to tidy this up.'

'Who?' asked Annie. A thought struck her. She

glanced back at her bedroom, then whispered, 'Not Gemma.'

'What?' said George.

Mitchell sighed. 'No, not Gemma. She wouldn't have access. And what would be in it for her?'

George considered. 'Revenge? They killed her son.'

'And that's why she's back?' said Mitchell. 'To stop the road, so her son's killers aren't freed.'

'It's mad,' said Annie. 'She wouldn't have.'

'No,' said Mitchell. 'Maybe not.'

'She did want to stop the road,' said George.

Annie tried to get her head round it. There just didn't seem to be an answer. And the more she thought about it, the more it seemed to sap her energy. That trip across town, and confronting the ghosts, had drained her.

She reached out a hand to steady herself with the wall.

The door of the bedroom creaked open, revealing Gemma. She stood tall and broad in the doorway, much more her old self. An imperious smile crept onto her features as they stared.

'Let them build the road,' she declared. 'Let them free the spirits. S'all in the past now. All long past.' She smiled – a little forced, but still a smile.

They gaped at her. She looked radiant, free of everything that had haunted her before.

'Now,' she said. 'You boys are hungry.'

*

Gemma clearly wanted to make an effort. She chatted to them as she conducted the pots and pans, a whirl of activity and salacious stories. The housemates sat at the table, amazed and entertained.

'You must see it all in the hospital,' she told George and Mitchell. 'It gets so nothing is surprising. You heard it all before. The terrible things people do to each other.'

'Where did you work?' Mitchell asked. He found himself grinning. Gemma had forgiven the kids who'd killed her son. Surely that was why she'd been brought back. They'd have one more meal and then there'd be a door to collect her.

'A few places,' said Gemma, busy rinsing the frozen peas in the sieve. 'They moved us round. They liked me as an assistant because I understood the names. Was doing a PhD until I got pregnant with Lee.' For a moment she froze, the sieve shaking in her hand. Then she took a deep breath, dumped the peas in a saucepan and dowsed them with cold water. 'But you meet a lot of characters, don't you?'

'Yeah,' said George, eager to move her on from thoughts of her son. 'There's this guy who turns up every Monday morning, wanting us to look at his fingers.'

As George made Annie and Gemma laugh with the story of Dirty Fingers Man, Mitchell considered what Gemma had said. She'd not gone silent because she'd mentioned Lee, but because of what she'd let slip.

She was a qualified pharmacist. And he'd been looking for someone who'd supplied dodgy drugs to the kids who'd hounded her son towards suicide.

Gemma tried to stop him leaving. She knew he wasn't meeting up with a guy called Dave at work; she knew he was on her heels. He'd been so stupid! She'd had the cause and the opportunity, and he just needed one last piece of evidence.

But he could play her at her own game.

'What else would I be doing?' he asked her, in front of Annie and George.

Gemma glared at him. 'I didn't say you'd be doing anything,' she pouted. 'You're just going out very late.'

'I'm nocturnal,' Mitchell told her. 'Haven't you seen any movies?' He grinned, George laughed and Gemma couldn't disagree,

'Watch her,' he told George – again in front of Gemma. 'She's had a rough day. Make sure she puts her feet up. And,' he added with emphasis, 'don't let her out of your sight.'

Annie reached over and grabbed Gemma's arm. 'We won't let her go anywhere,' she said.

It seemed such a cosy family, thought Mitchell, apart from the way Gemma glared at him with those beady eyes. He didn't like how sickly Annie seemed, either. The sooner he got this sorted out, the better.

When he reached the hospital, he had to go in

via A&E since all the other doors were locked. He traded banter with a few of the nurses and staff, all too busy to spot that he wasn't meant to be on duty. There was an envelope in his pigeon hole, addressed in spidery handwriting only to 'Porter, long hair, Irish accent.' It had been delivered by hand.

As he opened the envelope he recognised the scent, a perfume he'd smelled so recently. It contained a slip of paper, a computer print-out of an old photograph. A man of about 50 grinned impishly and raised a pint of beer. It took Mitchell a moment to recognise the late Mr Wright.

Mrs Wright knew it was silly, she said, but wanted to ask Mitchell to her husband's funeral the following Wednesday. 'He didn't want a service,' she said. 'So it's just a few drinks at the house. There won't be many people there. And I know you must hate these things. So I understand if you can't. But if you want to talk, you know where I am.'

Mitchell knew she was the one who needed conversation. It was pitiful, and he'd learnt early in his job not to get involved outside of the hospital wards and corridors. Perhaps that's what Mr Wright had done, and that was why the job had eaten him up. Mitchell couldn't say anything that would put her at ease, she just had to move on.

But nor could he make himself screw up the paper or throw it away. He wouldn't go anywhere near the woman, but he still pocketed the card. Anything else would have felt disrespectful.

Then he hurried upstairs to Intensive Care.

He stopped abruptly at the top of the stairs. There were people in the doorway to ICU. A man in jeans and a T-shirt held a stepladder steady while another man in similarly grubby clothes snooped around the ceiling. They weren't medical staff. Mitchell had never seen them before. But a lot of the repairs to the building got done at night to minimise inconvenience to the doctors.

'Hi,' he said as he approached. 'How's it going?'

'Slowly,' said the man holding the ladder. 'You know how many of these we've done?'

'No,' said Mitchell, looking up at the man's colleague, or at least at the legs that protruded from the square hatch in the ceiling. 'How many?'

The man holding the ladder considered. Numbers didn't seem his thing. 'Loads,' he said, at length.

'Wow,' said Mitchell. 'And will it make a difference?'

The man shrugged. 'Ours is not to reason why,' he said. 'Dr McGough wants CCTV on every ward, we give him CCTV on every ward.'

'Sure,' said Mitchell, though he felt suddenly cold. Again he felt that sense of being watched, like there was someone just a few steps ahead of him, seeing into his thoughts. He wouldn't show up on CCTV, and it would only be a matter of time before security noticed. His days at the hospital were over. He would have to move on.

But not yet, not before he'd completed his quest.

He hurried on into the low-lit ward, down the aisle of the sleeping dead. The girl on the night shift raised her head from her book. Mitchell grinned at her. Pretty girl. Dark hair, dark eyes, good skin. Probably wild in bed.

'Hey,' he said. 'You busy?'

She raised the book at him, a bulky paperback of a Victorian novel. 'Frantic,' she said.

'Good,' said Mitchell. 'Can I ask a favour?'

He explained that he wasn't meant to access the hospital database anyway – something the girl already knew. But, he said, he'd been trying to help out the Admin team, who were all under renewed pressure from Dr McGough to get through their backlog.

'He should take on more staff,' said the nurse.

Mitchell agreed with her wholeheartedly. 'But that's not going to happen,' he said. 'If they don't hit his target, they're going to be kicked out.'

'So you helped,' said the girl. She scratched at her neck, an unconscious move that drew attention to her exposed throat, the collarbone, the soft flesh. Mitchell felt the darkness welling inside him, the raw desire to feed. He licked his lips, and she seemed to take that to mean he fancied her. She smiled.

'Yeah,' said Mitchell. 'But I think I may have entered something wrong. Can you look something up for me, make sure it's all as it should be?'

The girl considered. Her breathing had quickened, he could hear her heart pulsing. He tried not to let himself see the ripeness of her skin.

'All right,' she said. 'But quickly.'

He hurried round to join her in front of the computer. She logged in and he told her the name to look up: Gemma Romain. There was only one match, born Christmas Day 1957, died 29 September 1999.

'It's an old one,' said the nurse.

'Yeah,' said Mitchell. 'I didn't add anything, did I?'

The nurse opened up the file. They read through the details. Gemma had gone through several doses of chemotherapy from 1995. She'd responded well to begin with, but then the cancer had clawed its way back. Mitchell recalled that Lee had died at the end of June 1999, by which time, the notes said, Gemma had been confined to bed. She had not recovered. In late August, just trying to walk to the toilet she'd had a nasty fall, breaking her arm. She'd not got out of bed again.

Mitchell stared at the notes. Gemma couldn't have made the amphetamine mixture that had killed her son's tormentors. She would have been too weak.

'No,' said the nurse. 'This file's not been amended since two days after she died. You're in the clear.'

She logged out of the system. Mitchell thanked her and let her get back to her book. He made his way slowly back up the ward, to where the two men with the stepladder were fixing the black globe which would keep watch on the sleepers.

As he passed, he glanced at Rebecca Hywel-Jones and the machines that kept her alive. In the tomb-like darkness he almost didn't spot the skinny boy sat beside her. The boy got to his feet as he saw Mitchell looking at him. His eyes opened wide, in fear. The same expression Mitchell had seen on the face of the boy's mother.

'Lee,' he said. And the boy faded into the air.

'You say something?' said the man at the ladder as Mitchell passed.

'Not really,' said Mitchell. 'You almost done?'

'Yeah,' said the man. 'Another hour or so. You think we'll catch any villains?'

Mitchell didn't answer.

He couldn't go back to the house. He couldn't face how Gemma would love the fact that he had failed. Mitchell knew he was missing something, that there had to be an answer. He couldn't believe Gemma was innocent.

He followed the street towards Bristol town centre, and the noise and light of the pubs. Then he saw the turning for Ashton Park and followed that without really thinking, finding himself at Bryn Road almost by surprise.

It seemed different in the darkness. The rain had stopped and the air felt fresh and cool after the day's downpour. There were lights on in numbers 9 and 6. A grubby face peered out at him from number 6, and Mitchell waved cheerily at Ian.

Ian waved back. 'Coming in?' he asked Mitchell. 'We've got some wine.'

'No,' said Mitchell. 'Just wanted to see how you're doing.'

'Good,' said Ian.

'Good,' said Mitchell. 'Well, I'll look in on the others.'

Ian tapped a finger to his temple, a kind of salute, and disappeared back into the house. Mitchell waited, seeing if anyone else would look out on him. Then he turned to number 8.

He stepped through the open doorway into the dark orifice of the house, the stench of abandonment reaching out to him. He'd spent nights in worse places and had nothing to fear. Yet he found his senses screaming as he made his way inside.

Stairs led up in front of him. The living room stretched to the back of the house, and a kitchen with a hatchway beside the door. The furniture and anything of value had long since been looted, and the dark carpet was blotchy with holes. Floorboards creaked under his tread. He could feel them watching.

'Hey,' he said. And they came for him.

He didn't see them at first. They whispered around him, brushing against his skin. Then he could see the streak of pale of blue light as they passed by. Just as Annie had said, there was barely anything left of the three ghosts. Their eyes were blank, their faces bloated, their bodies tapered away to nothing below the hip. Another month, another week, and he might have missed them. Perhaps that was why they had acted, calling Gemma back through the door. Or perhaps she had known the new road demolishing the house would release them, or help someone piece together her secret.

He recognised Chantell Roy from the picture in her file, a pretty girl with gold rings in her ears. The boy to her left must have been Barry Jones. Thomas Ho floated forward, mouth hanging open ready to howl. After all this time on their own, the ghosts had lost their ability to speak. Mitchell had seen it before, had fretted that this eerie fate might have been Annie's had he and George not been able to help her.

'You want to move on,' he said. 'I know. I can help.'

The ghosts gaped at him, shimmering in the darkness.

'I just want to know a few things. Why isn't Lee here, too? What's keeping him away?'

The ghosts stared blankly back at him. Thomas Ho's mouth twitched. He made no sound, but when he repeated the gesture, Mitchell could just about read the two syllables from his blackened lips.

'Party,' said Mitchell.

Thomas Ho nodded, a spasm that twitched his whole body.

'You had a party,' said Mitchell, piecing it together. 'After Lee died. A few months after Lee died.' He smiled, understanding. 'An exorcism,' he said. 'You had a party to clear the air.'

Thomas Ho nodded.

'And it worked,' said Mitchell. 'He's been stuck outside ever since.'

Mitchell stuck his hands in his pockets to find a cigarette. 'There's still one thing I can't get my head round,' he said. He pulled out the cigarettes and something else as well, a folded piece of paper. 'You must have got the drugs from someone. You got a botched supply. That can't have been a coincidence.'

Thomas Ho twitched, his head twisted left and right as if it were about to fall from his shoulders.

'No,' agreed Mitchell. He lit his cigarette and inhaled the needed warmth. The ghosts seemed to hover around him, as if warming themselves round the tiny light. No, he realised, they warmed themselves round him, drawing strength even from a vampire.

'You got the drugs from someone. Someone who knew what they'd do. Someone murdered you all.'

Thomas Ho shimmered closer, an arm raised towards Mitchell. There was a pinprick of light in his hollow, dark eyes, a glimmer that had not been there before. Mitchell could feel the ghosts drawing strength, leeching it from him.

'We,' rasped Thomas in a terrible parody of a human voice. 'Deserved. It.'

Mitchell shook his head. 'No. You bullied Lee,

I know that. But there was also his mum. There's something about his mum.'

Thomas sighed, and Mitchell felt the faint breath on his face. 'We deserved it,' he insisted hoarsely.

'Maybe,' said Mitchell. 'But this has gone on long enough. Who gave you the drugs? Who did you buy them from?'

Thomas said nothing. He still had his arm out, his fingers stretching to Mitchell, pleading. It looked like the ghosts had no idea.

And then Mitchell realised what Thomas was trying to reach for. Mitchell held the folded paper that he'd found his pocket. Thomas nodded, his face twisting into a grotesque smile. The other ghosts around him sighed.

Mitchell unfolded the paper, already knowing whose face he would see.

Chapter
THIRTEEN

George yawned. It was eleven o'clock. 'I'm going to have to go to bed,' he said, stretching.

'You don't want to finish the game?' Gemma asked him.

'Sorry,' he said. 'I've got work.'

'And you're still worried about your job.'

'Uh, yeah,' said George. 'Well, not worried. But I want to be fresh.'

'They'll have made their minds up anyhow,' said Gemma. 'Too late to change anything. Finish the game.'

George pushed his fingers up underneath his glasses so he could rub his eyes. 'No,' he said. 'I'm going to bed.'

'Another five minutes,' said Gemma. 'That won't make any difference.'

'Oh, let him go to bed,' snapped Annie. George and Gemma both turned to her in surprise. 'I mean,' said Annie, more gently. 'If he wants to go to bed he can.'

George stared at Annie, but he knew why she was bristling. Gemma had forgiven the people who'd killed her son, and now her story was over. A door would come for her and she'd be gone, at peace for evermore. And Annie envied that, or feared it. She'd ignored the doors for herself, and seemed stuck in this house. He could see the tension in Annie: she didn't like the waiting; maybe she just wanted the door to come and it all to be over.

George, meanwhile, didn't like what he'd seen on Mitchell's face. George knew he hadn't fed in a couple of days, what with the new regime making it difficult to get to the packets of blood. He knew he should trust Mitchell, he knew he shouldn't worry. But he couldn't help it. And sitting down here, pretending to play games, just made him want to scream.

Gemma nodded, her bottom lip sticking out in a sulk. 'Nobody forcing him to play if he don't want to,' she said. 'Nobody forcing anyone.'

'I'm just tired,' said George, getting to his feet. 'You can finish the game without me, or we can pick it up tomorrow.'

'Sure,' said Gemma, folding her arms. 'It's your house.'

'Gemma,' said George.

'Go to bed, George,' said Annie, glaring at Gemma. 'She's just cross you won't do what she wants.'

'What *I* want?' Gemma gasped. 'I don't want anything! You're the ones that need feeding and entertaining. I cooked that meal for you!'

'And very nice it was, too,' said George, trying to stop the women from having a fight. 'But if I don't go to bed now I'll get scratchy.' He grinned. 'And you wouldn't like me when I'm scratchy.'

Gemma nodded. 'I might not be here tomorrow,' she said.

'No,' said George, 'I suppose not.' And he sat back down again.

Annie, too, was subdued by Gemma's statement. She reached forward for the dice.

'Of course he told me,' she said. 'I was his wife.'

Mitchell sat at the counter in Mrs Wright's kitchen while she poured tea from a pot in a knitted cosy. She was one of those people who poured the milk first, but Mitchell didn't say anything. He didn't know what to make of her, or the poise with which she accepted that he knew her secret. She had been expecting this moment for such a long time; and with her husband dead she had nothing left to lose. He almost thought she welcomed his confronting her.

'He told you everything,' he said.

'We discussed it,' said Mrs Wright, passing over his cup and saucer. Mitchell peered down at the pale tea and she smiled. 'It's perfectly safe,' she said. 'I'll take a sip from it if you don't believe me.'

'You might not want to survive,' Mitchell told her.

She smiled. 'True. So don't drink it.' She sipped her own tea just to needle him. He knew there weren't many poisons that would affect him, so he took the risk. That show of trust in her would let him ask his questions.

'There was this woman dying of cancer,' he said.

'Gemma Romain,' said Mrs Wright. 'I never met her. But she'd gone through an abhorrent series of treatments and she knew it wasn't working.'

'And then her son died.'

'Selfish little soul,' said Mrs Wright, her lips pursing with distaste. 'His mum is dying and he's all she's got in the world. But he doesn't want to go home.'

Mitchell sighed. 'I don't think she was always easy to live with. He was probably depressed, a long-term thing.'

Mrs Wright conceded the point. 'I think my husband was rather in thrall to Ms Romain. She seemed to get whatever she wanted.'

'Yeah,' said Mitchell with feeling.

She looked up at him, surprised.

'I can imagine,' he added.

'So her son was living in this filthy squat down in Ashton Park,' Mrs Wright went on. 'There were drugs and who knows what. The police could never do anything, and the news people didn't want to know.' She stopped, taking another sip of her tea. When she spoke again, her voice was softer, less sure. 'At least, that's what Ms Romain told Jim.'

'She said they'd killed her son,' nodded Mitchell.

'No, she said he'd killed himself. But because of what they'd done. Selling drugs to children. No, handing them out for free so the children would be hooked. Then they'd have to pay when they wanted more.'

Mitchell held Mrs Wright's gaze. 'That's what she told you.'

'But Jim had seen it!' Mrs Wright declared. 'He'd worked the Friday nights, seen the kids being brought in. Not even 10 years old, and they were coughing up blood! The things he brought home with him sometimes... Well, you must have seen it yourself.'

'I've seen a few things,' Mitchell admitted. 'And you want to do something.'

Mrs Wright nodded. 'And then you're given the chance,' she said.

'Ms Romain suggested it,' said Mitchell.

'No,' said Mrs Wright, then hesitated. 'Jim thought it was his idea. But now you ask, I'm not so sure. He was a good man.'

'You thought you were saving those kids,' said Mitchell.

'Yes,' said Mrs Wright. 'He got Ms Romain to tell us what to do. You can make up the stuff from household bits and pieces. The tricky thing is red phosphorous, which is usually illegal. But they use it in all sorts of industrial processes. Ms Romain supplied us with a contact. You know she was a chemist.'

'I'd guessed,' said Mitchell.

'We were just following her instructions,' said Mrs Wright. 'Brewed up the batch here. You wouldn't believe the stink.'

'An industrial sort of smell,' said Mitchell. 'Acrid and tangy, like it's burning the hair in your nostrils.'

'Yes,' said Mrs Wright, surprised. 'You've done your homework.'

Mitchell nodded, thinking of the industrial tang in the air, whenever he'd been near Gemma. It wafted around her, a reminder of all that she'd done.

'A lot of the tablets didn't come out right,' Mrs Wright continued. 'But we had enough for our purpose. I drove him to the house. We waited until one of them came out. Asian boy, in a long black coat and safety pins. He wore these huge platform boots. I remember those. Dressing up like some kind of monster. Why would an ordinary, decent person ever wear something like that?'

Mitchell nodded. 'You offered him the first batch for free.'

'We were playing him at his own game,' said Mrs Wright. 'We told him to share them around his colleagues. Test the quality of our wares. We didn't tell him to throw a party.'

'They'd been through a lot, in that house. Lee had killed himself, they all blamed themselves. You let them forget that for a while.'

Mrs Wright looked down at the tea things, not seeing them. Mitchell hadn't meant to be cruel. The awful thing was that he understood exactly what she'd done. He had seen the young kids brought in, seen the doctors and nurses try everything to save them. And it wasn't just the very young children: teenagers, kids in their twenties, even older. They were all so young to Mitchell, frittering away their existence for the sake of a few cheap thrills.

'We thought we'd get the ringleaders,' said Mrs Wright gently. 'We thought we'd stop them in their tracks. And it would be a warning to anyone else targeting kids.'

'Except they weren't selling drugs,' said Mitchell.

'No,' said Mrs Wright.

Mitchell waited for her to carry on, but she just stared down at the tea things.

'Was he working when they came into A&E?' he asked.

Mrs Wright didn't appear to have heard him. Then she shook her head. 'No,' she said. 'He had a shift the next day, by which time the two boys were dead. The girls, I think, survived a bit longer.'

'One of them's still in a coma,' said Mitchell.

Mrs Wright looked up at him, horrified. 'No,' she whispered.

'It's been ten years, but she's still going. Her notes don't link her to any of the others.'

Mrs Wright dabbed at her eyes with a hankie she kept in her sleeve. 'Jim went to see Ms Romain. She'd set us up. Of course these kids weren't what she'd made out. They weren't dealers, they were just kids themselves.'

'But she was slipping away,' said Mitchell.

'Died a fortnight later, a smile on her face. She'd dumped us in it. We couldn't go to the police. We had to protect ourselves. We'd acted in good faith!'

Mitchell didn't disagree with her. After a moment he said, 'Someone edited the notes on the hospital database, so the four kids weren't connected.'

Mrs Wright shrugged. 'Jim just erased the connections. Isolated incidents aren't worth following up. But he got caught on the system. They thought he was gawping at naked bodies!'

'But he couldn't say what he'd really been doing,' said Mitchell.

'No,' said Mrs Wright. 'They let him retire. And he walked out of the hospital after all those years' service. There wasn't even a do in the pub.'

'You got away with it,' said Mitchell.

Mrs Wright stared at him. 'No,' she said. 'He never got away from it. We'd go to the cinema or for dinner somewhere, and he'd get up in the middle. He'd think he'd seen Ms Romain's son. Last week I heard him shouting, telling Lee to look in the house, to see what we'd done for his sake. And then three days ago....' She tailed off, reaching again for the tissue in her sleeve.

Mitchell already knew what had happened. Mr Wright had been visited by a ghost and the shock had killed him. But this time it hadn't been Lee.

'So,' said Mrs Wright. 'That's everything.'

'No,' said Mitchell. 'It's just the start.'

'You must tell the authorities,' said Mrs Wright. 'It'll be a relief. It's been a relief just telling you. I think I knew, when I first saw you. There was something in the air.'

Mitchell stared back at her. Mrs Wright hadn't asked him the obvious question. He couldn't go to the police or to Dr McGough without them asking how he'd pieced this together. They wouldn't be happy with any answer he could give them. He'd only single himself out. And the only way Mitchell could ever survive among the humans was to remain invisible.

'I have to go,' he said, getting down from his stool.

'But you'll tell them,' she said, eager to be convicted.

He didn't say anything. There was nothing he could do, not without endangering himself – and George and Annie, too. He wasn't being selfish, he told himself.

And anyway, Mrs Wright would have her reckoning one day. She'd be judged by the things that lurked in the darkness on the other side of death. He wondered how her husband was faring.

Mitchell walked away.

He walked out of her house and across the front patio and out the little gate. For a moment he stood on the street, feeling safe.

Then he turned to the pale blue figure beside him.

As he watched, as it drew strength from his attention, the pale luminescence took shape, picking out features – a T-shirt, bare arms, a long, thin neck and head. The ghost of a gaunt, skinny teenager stared balefully at Mitchell. He raised his eyebrows in greeting.

'Lee,' he said. 'We need to talk about your mother.'

Chapter
FOURTEEN

The front door burst open, the force of it making them all jump. Mitchell strode in, hair strewn by the wind outside.

'Where's Gemma?' he demanded of Annie and George. 'I told you not to let her out of your sight.'

She appeared from the kitchen with a saucepan. 'I was making hot milk,' she said. And the pan dropped from her hands and clattered at her feet.

'I brought a friend,' said Mitchell, ushering forward the skinny black teenager who held Gemma's awestruck gaze.

Lee and Gemma stared at one another, mouths both hanging open. Mitchell glanced round, grinning at George and Annie.

Annie stepped forward to join Mitchell, closing

the front door behind him, sealing them all inside. She looked from Lee, the gaunt black boy, to his statuesque mother. And she saw Gemma glaring back with the same disappointment with which she'd looked on Annie. There were tears in Lee's eyes. And yet he shimmered, so wan she could see right through him.

'Say something,' Annie pleaded of Gemma. 'He must have waited so long.'

'Where?' sniffed Gemma. 'On the streets?'

Lee opened his mouth to speak. No sound came out. His mouth just hung open.

'Forgotten how to talk,' said Gemma as if it were all she had ever expected of him. 'Got nothing to say to your mum?'

Lee closed his mouth, still staring right at her. Then he shook his head.

Gemma tried not to show how much it affected her. She took a tiny step backwards, and Annie saw that her hands were trembling.

'You're scared of him,' said Annie.

Gemma scowled at her. 'I'm his mother,' she said. 'I gave up everything for this boy.'

'And then,' said Mitchell, 'he became a man.'

Gemma didn't say anything; she just stared at Lee.

Annie thought he might have changed somehow. It took her a moment to realise that he didn't shimmer as he had, and she could barely see through him now. There was the door, and then there it wasn't.

He had come back from the brink.

'What was it?' asked Mitchell. 'Did he remind you too much of his father?'

'He never had a father,' snapped Gemma.

Lee opened his mouth and let out a strangled sound. The croak twisted, becoming a parody of words. 'He didn't leave me,' he told Gemma. 'He left you.'

Gemma shook her head. 'No,' she said.

'He said,' Lee continued, 'you sucked the life from him.'

'He never made time for you,' said Gemma. 'He was never there.'

Lee smiled an awful smile. 'After he left,' he said, 'I saw him all the time. He was the one who told me I had to move back in with you.'

Gemma stared at him aghast. Her mouth twitched, the shape of the word *no*, but she made no sound.

'You've been with him for the last ten years,' said Annie.

Lee shook his shoulders as he shook his head. 'He moved on. Took his new family away. They're happy.'

Annie reached her hand out to him instinctively. He felt cold. 'And you've been without anyone all that time?' she said. 'Out on the street. No one even knowing you were there.'

Lee nodded.

'What changed?' asked Mitchell.

'The road,' said Lee. 'I felt the road they were

building, and my house in its way. I made myself go to look at it, while I could.' He let out a long breath, a sigh. 'I was happy there.'

'They bullied you!' said Gemma. 'They sent me pictures of what they'd done.'

Lee twitched, a rough approximation of a shrug. 'A game,' he said. 'A forfeit.'

Gemma shook her head. 'They were never your friends. People like that.'

'They were worse than me,' said Lee. 'When I came back to the house. They were inside, wasting away. They couldn't keep me out.'

'And you saw what your mother had done,' said Mitchell.

Lee nodded.

All eyes turned to Gemma, and in that moment she seemed to regain some of her earlier steel. She glared back at her son, her eyes burning bright.

'I did it for you,' she told him. 'I got them back. They were the ones who killed you.'

'They didn't kill me,' said Lee, without any hint of menace. His steady tone made it all the more terrifying. 'They were all I had.'

Gemma gaped at him, appalled. 'You ungrateful wretch!'

'Yes,' he said. 'I shouldn't have done what I did. And I've been punished. But what you did...' He took a step towards her, his arm outstretched. He opened his fingers wide, as if he were going to offer her a blessing. It seemed to Annie as if the tips of his

238

fingers shone with silver light.

And that she could see through Gemma to the wallpaper beyond.

'No,' said Gemma. 'I loved you like no one else could.'

'You protected me,' said Lee. 'You guided me. You only wanted the best.'

'Yes,' said Gemma, her voice fading into the air. 'Yes.'

'You sapped the life from me. The house was my escape.'

'You left me,' wailed Gemma.

'I couldn't breathe,' said Lee. 'I needed space away. And then you got worse. You were dying. And I had to come back to look after you.'

Gemma stared at him. Annie covered her eyes with her hand, trying to shield the light of Lee. There was so little of Gemma left, a shadow against the wall. But enough to be hurt by her son's words. 'That's why…' she said.

And there was nothing left of her. Just a sigh hanging in the air.

'You chose your own road,' said Lee. 'We all do.'

George stared at the space where Gemma had been, then turned to face Lee, standing tall. He felt dazed. He could see Annie and Mitchell were dazed too, blinded by the light that Lee held in his outstretched hand.

'Um,' said George. 'What did you just do?'

'Sapped her strength,' said Mitchell. 'What she'd always done. Even when she was alive.'

George gaped. 'He zapped her?'

'No,' said Lee impassively. 'She's still there.'

'What?' said Annie, horrified.

'He just took her strength,' said Mitchell. 'She'll be like he was. Unfixed. Ungrounded. Just an echo in the air.'

'That's awful!' said Annie. 'He pulled a thread and she just came apart.' She hugged her cardigan round her, as if to hold herself together.

'That is a bit sick,' said George, backing away from Lee. Lee continued to stand there, arm outstretched, staring at the place which had just been his mum.

'He found out what she'd done,' said Mitchell.

Lee turned to Annie and George. 'She convinced a man to murder my friends, and one who has not yet died. And she killed the man himself.'

'What?' said Annie. 'How?'

'It's a long story,' said Mitchell. 'But I don't have time to tell it now. I've got to get back to the hospital.'

'What?' said George. 'Wait a minute. Mitchell!'

Mitchell was already through the front door. 'Got to dash,' he grinned at them. 'Don't wait up.' And he was gone again.

George turned to Annie. 'Where—' he began.

Annie was no longer there. Nor was Lee. George stood entirely alone in the house.

*

Mitchell wasn't surprised to find Lee and Annie waiting for him as he reached the Intensive Care ward. He didn't say anything, just poked his head round the corner.

The beds lay still in the darkness, machines twittering softly, lights flickering as they kept the sleepers alive. At the end of the aisle of beds, Mitchell could just make out the nurse he'd spoken to earlier that evening. She sat back in her chair, head tilted back, mouth hanging open as she slept.

Mitchell glanced back at Lee and Annie. Neither of them were there. He looked round to find them both standing at the bed of Rebecca Hywel-Jones.

He looked up and to his right, at the small black sphere that protruded from the ceiling. It gave no indication which way the camera was looking, but Mitchell risked pressing himself through the door into the ward. It moved as he squeezed past, but he hoped anyone watching would think it was a draft, perhaps from the air conditioning.

Mitchell crept on tiptoes down the ward to where the ghosts were waiting. With Lee and Annie stood the ghosts of Thomas Ho, Chantell Roy and Barry Jones. They stared balefully at Mitchell as he approached. Lee and Annie were the only ones not to raise their hands, to bask in Mitchell's warmth.

Lee and Thomas and Barry had done this for Chantell the previous Sunday. They had ended the torment, let her move on to the next level. He assumed that had rung a bell somewhere, in the place beyond death, and Gemma had known her secret had been found out. However she'd done it, whatever deal she'd struck, she'd come back to ensure no one could piece together what she'd done.

He still didn't know why she'd turned up in his house. Perhaps Annie had forged some link with the world beyond by declining to pass through. Perhaps there was something more sinister at work.

The ghosts were in no state to battle with Gemma – they'd kept out of her way while they could. It had taken all the energy they possessed to switch off Chantell's machines, it had almost unravelled them. They'd had no one else to draw strength from until Mitchell had dared to see them.

Mitchell looked at them now. Lee looked strong enough from what he'd taken from his mother. Or had he shared some of that strength with the others? They shimmered, translucent, just echoes of the people they'd been. They still needed his help.

He didn't say anything, he didn't pause to consider. Mitchell reached over to the machine beside the sleeping girl, and clicked off the power.

Several things happened at once. The machines stopped twittering. The lights fell dead. The system cried out an electronic tone of distress. The nurse at the desk started out of her sleep, and turned to look in the direction of the noise. And Annie, Lee and the other ghosts all hurled themselves at Mitchell.

*

'Didn't know we'd be able to carry you,' Annie told Mitchell. 'Lucky we did.'

George found them cluttering up the living room: Annie, George and five shimmering ghosts in their teens. 'I was going to go to bed,' he told them. 'But there doesn't seem much point now. Are you going to tell me what's happened?'

Annie made George and Mitchell tea.

'You killed her?' said George, incredulous, as Mitchell tried to explain what they'd done.

'But no one will see me on the CCTV,' grinned Mitchell. 'It's the perfect crime.'

'But you killed her!' said George. 'Who are you to decide?' He had views about this sort of thing. Once they'd been strictly held, religious views. They still raised a passion inside him.

A slender hand touched his shoulder. George turned to face a dazzlingly beautiful woman in her late twenties. She glowed with silver light.

'It's what I wanted,' she said. 'Trust me.'

George tried to say something, that it still wasn't right, but his brain was capsizing. The beautiful girl put a finger to his lips.

'Now we can move on,' she said.

'Yes,' was all George could say. He followed the ghosts out of the living room, to find them passing one by one through a door that shouldn't have been there. The beautiful girl reached up on tiptoe to kiss his cheek, then scurried after the others. George found himself smiling. After all that they suffered, they showed no bitterness. They were serene and shimmering, like angels.

Lee went last. He stood just in front of the door that shouldn't have been there, and turned back to look one last time at George and Mitchell and Annie. His face was impassive, no hint of emotion in his eyes. He looked at Annie.

'They're not finished with you,' he told her. And then he stepped through the door. The door that shouldn't have been there, that wasn't, that had never been.

'What did he mean?' George asked Annie, draping an arm around her.

She hugged him close, squeezed him tightly. But she didn't answer.

Chapter
FIFTEEN

'And that's it?' said Gavin Foot. 'That's all you can give me?'

'The girl died,' shrugged Mitchell. 'Isn't that enough?'

They had met outside the offices of the *Daily Press*. Mitchell didn't have long, he explained. He just wanted to give Gavin the details and be gone. But rather than sorting everything out, his answers only provoked more questions. Gavin was good. He was conscientious. And Albert the vampire had been right – he was dangerous.

'What about the records being changed?' said Gavin. 'How can we explain that?'

'Incompetence,' said Mitchell. 'Human error.' Gavin shook his head, laughing at the absurdity. 'What?' said Mitchell. 'You think there's a conspiracy?

These kids took some kind of amphetamine that scrambled their insides. That's what killed them. Everything else is just down to a bit of misfiling.'

'The database here was changed, too,' said Gavin. 'Someone didn't want us to piece this thing together.'

Mitchell didn't have an answer. Well, he did: Lee and maybe the others had deleted the file and then sent a note to the editor. They'd tried to get their story noticed, so they could draw strength from the attention. But he couldn't share any of that with Gavin.

'I've given you what I've got,' said Mitchell. 'Is it enough for your story?'

Gavin ran a hand through his thinning hair. 'Yes,' he admitted. 'I can work it up into something. Thank you.'

'No worries,' said Mitchell.

'But there's still more there,' said Gavin. 'It's just the tip of what's been going on.'

Mitchell shrugged. 'I need to head back.'

They shook hands, an oddly old-fashioned gesture and yet very Gavin all the same. Mitchell started down the pavement, lighting a cigarette. Gavin called after him.

'Mitchell! You've got an idea, haven't you? About who got into the files.'

Mitchell grinned back at him. 'Honestly?' he said. 'Ghosts.'

Gavin stared at him for a moment, like he thought

it just possible. Then he shook his head, laughing, and went inside to write up his story.

George was scratchy with people at work, but otherwise the day passed without incident. He got home and flopped on the sofa, and Annie brought him his dinner to eat in front of the telly. Mitchell joined them and they watched some nature programme about some endangered parrots in New Zealand.

Annie cried. George put his arms round her. Mitchell opened another bottle of wine.

George and Mitchell made their way into work together the next morning, and George felt they'd got past yet another ordeal. They were going to be OK.

'Oh hell,' said Mitchell as they arrived at the main entrance of the hospital on Little Guinea Street, and the alcove where the smokers congregated. There were no smokers to be seen, no cigarette butts on the floor.

They hurried on into the hospital, through the waiting room where patients sat waiting, into the treatment bays where no one was being treated. A posh voice could be heard down the corridor in the mess room. George and Mitchell raced down to join the throng.

'Is this,' said the voice they recognised only too well, '*really* the road you want to take?'

The room was heaving with bodies, all the staff that could spare the time to be here. Consultants, junior doctors, nurses and cleaning staff – George could see representatives of all the ranks. All in rapt silence as Dr Declan McGough strained to keep his temper.

'I am *very* disappointed,' he told them. 'I wanted to do this together. We *thrive* when we work together. But someone here, perhaps one of you in this room, is working on their own.'

He brandished a folded newspaper as if it were a weapon. 'I have already complained to the editor about this Gavin Foot,' he said. George glanced at Mitchell, who watched Dr McGough with a sly smile on his face.

'I have underlined,' McGough continued, 'that our new CCTV system did not cause a short circuit, and did not kill that girl! And I have asked – no *demanded* – that he share with me *who* would have *dared* to say otherwise!'

He threw the newspaper to the floor amongst some of the consultants. It skidded across the floor between them. There were yelps of alarm, and laughter. The noise died down almost instantly with one look from Dr McGough.

He stood there before them, quaking with fury, his cheeks glowing scarlet and sweat beading on his forehead. George watched him taking deep breaths, perhaps reciting some mantra for keeping his cool. He recognised the symptoms of a man struggling with his anger.

Dr McGough reached one hand up to smooth the overly greased flank of hair that lay across his bald forehead. He smoothed it again, then lowered his hand, surreptitiously wiping his palm on the side of his jacket.

'We will be dismantling the additional surveillance equipment,' he said with quiet fury, 'pending independent findings. The new administration wing in the old isolation wards will have to be put on hold while the budget is reworked. And the rest of my day is to be taken up with Her Majesty's press.

'Not a good start,' he told them. 'Not a good start.'

And then he looked right at George and Mitchell.

'I'll be watching.'

'You gave that story to Gavin,' George whispered as the ranks broke up and headed back to work.

Mitchell shrugged. 'He needed something. Had this thing in his head about someone going around changing patient records. Don't, I told him, put anything down to conspiracy when it can be put down to incompetence.'

He laughed, but George didn't laugh with him. George, Mitchell had noticed, really didn't know how to relax. He tried to explain this to him as they made their way up to the locker rooms. But George shrugged him off and went his own way.

Mitchell sighed. And a woman called out his name.

He turned, to find Gail coming towards him. He grinned, but she didn't grin back. She looked deadly serious.

'You've not got the blame for the girl who died,' said Mitchell.

Gail shook her head. 'Wasn't the one on duty,' she said. 'And anyway – electrical fault.'

'Right,' said Mitchell. 'Good.'

'No, not good,' said Gail. 'We've got to test all the equipment and have it approved. Means I lose the weekend.'

'Oh,' said Mitchell. 'Sorry.'

'What have you got to be sorry for?' she asked.

He grinned. 'Nothing. Sorry.'

Gail stared up at him, her eyes blazing with anger – and also something else.

'What?' he asked.

'I thought you'd want to know,' said Gail. 'Mrs Wright. The lady you put in a taxi the other day…'

'Yeah, I remember,' said Mitchell.

'Killed herself,' said Gail.

'What?' said Mitchell.

'Hanged herself, they said. Guess she couldn't go on without her husband. Think I sort of respect that.'

Mitchell didn't say anything. He hoped Mrs Wright had found some kind of peace. But he knew in his heart that something else probably awaited.

'You all right?' asked Gail.

'Yeah,' said Mitchell. 'Sorry.'

'Stop saying that!'

'What?' said Mitchell. 'Oh sure. Sorry.'

Gail slapped his shoulder. 'You're so stupid,' she said, though she was smiling. 'You should be more like George.'

'We should all be more like George,' said Mitchell. 'The world would be a better place. You like him, don't you?'

Gail stepped away from him. 'Me and Kaz haven't decided yet.'

Mitchell nodded. This was exactly what George needed: a couple of girls who liked him but who came with strings. Consenting adults, no one got hurt. Perfect cure for all ills.

'No pressure,' he said. 'But why don't you come round to the house sometime?'

They cooked together. Whatever their worries about work or the future or all the things they'd been through, they were forgotten in the kitchen. George decided ingredients and Annie's job was the opening. Mitchell pinched her sides as she opened the tin of Flageolet kidney beans, so she threw bean juice all over the kitchen. Even George laughed, then skidded back on the wet floor.

They were giggling, bickering, enjoying a rare evening when the sky didn't seem poised to fall, and the front door bell rang.

'You better get that,' Annie told Mitchell.

'Let George,' he said. 'I expect it's for him.'

'What?' said George, busy stirring things in the saucepans. 'Why'd it ever be for me?'

'You get visitors,' said Mitchell.

'About once a year,' said George, shoving him out of the kitchen.

'Has it been that long already?' asked Mitchell, as he moved through the living room and opened the front door.

'Kaz!' he said.

Standing in the street, under a rainbow umbrella – despite the complete and total absence of rain – was Kaz. Her face was flushed, and she looked as if she'd been running.

Kaz did a funny little dance as she struggled to catch her breath and said something that sounded like 'Jaw'.

'Jaw?' echoed Mitchell.

'George,' said Kaz, more clearly this time.

'Mitchell,' beamed Mitchell.

'No. George. Where is he?' said Kaz. 'Need to see George. He's…'

Mitchell watched her take another big, gulping breath.

'George is going to be a daddy!' she told him.

Acknowledgements

Albert and Steve for providing a door; Mark and James for covering fire; the cast and crew of *Being Human* for even laying on a car; the real Gemma Romain for becoming a monster; Debbie Challis and Alex Wilcock for spotting wrongness; Bristol boys Bryn and Gobber for native wisdom.

Also available from BBC Books

being human
CHASERS

by Mark Michalowski

ISBN 978 1 846 07899 6   £7.99

George's friend, Kaz, arrives at the flat with a staggering request: she and her partner Gail want to have a child, and they'd like George to be the father. George is warming to the idea – he's always wanted kids, and he can be as involved in the baby's life as he wishes – but he is wary: what if his condition is genetic?

Mitchell and Annie don't approve of the new plan, but Mitchell is wrestling with a difficult decision of his own. A patient at the hospital, Leo, is surprisingly good company for a pasty older bloke who believes the 1980s were a golden age. But he seems a little too interested in Mitchell's history – and he has a surprising request of his own in store for his new friend...

Featuring Mitchell, George and Annie, as played by Aidan Turner, Russell Tovey and Lenora Crichlow in the hit series created by Toby Whithouse for BBC Television.

Also available from BBC Books

being human
BAD BLOOD

by James Goss

ISBN 978 1 846 07900 9   £7.99

One of Annie's oldest friends has come looking for her – and what's more amazing is that she's found her. Denise is the ultimate party girl, and she's determined to bring Annie out of her shell. Mitchell is delighted, but George really thinks the last thing they need to do is to go out and meet new people.

Annie and Denise throw themselves into organising a Bingo night at the local sports hall – after all, it's for charity, and what's not to love about having a good time? But why is Denise back in town? Why have Bristol's vampires suddenly started hanging around wherever they go? And why does George get the feeling that Bingo night is going to go horribly, horribly wrong?

Featuring Mitchell, George and Annie, as played by Aidan Turner, Russell Tovey and Lenora Crichlow in the hit series created by Toby Whithouse for BBC Television.